"What are you doing?"
Senetra whispered.

"Going out of my mind."

When she didn't move away, Alex leaned forward and kissed her lightly on the lips, expecting her to either jerk away or punch him. One taste of her was worth a punch in the gut.

When she still didn't move, he gathered her in his arms and ran his tongue against the seam of her lips. She opened for him, allowing his first taste of pure bliss.

Pulling her onto his lap, he stroked her tongue with his, sucking gently. He caressed her slowly, starting with her arms, moving down to her waist and hips. Her sweet moans drove him wild. When he touched her thigh he felt her hands tentatively stroke him in return. A blaze heated his blood so hot he thought he'd burn from pure need. He couldn't get enough of her.

Books by Candice Poarch

Kimani Romance

Sweet Southern Comfort
His Tempest
Then Comes Love
Loving Spoonful
Safe in His Embrace

Kimani Arabesque

Family Bonds
Loving Delilah
Courage Under Fire
Lighthouse Magic
Bargain of the Heart
The Last Dance
'Tis the Season
Shattered Illusions
Tender Escape
Intimate Secrets
A Mother's Touch
The Essence of Love
With This Kiss
Moonlight and Mistletoe
White Lightning

CANDICE POARCH

fell in love with stories centered upon romance and families many years ago. She feels the quest for love is universal. She portrays a sense of community and mutual support in her novels. In 2010 Candice released her twenty-third novel.

Candice grew up in Stony Creek, Virginia, south of Richmond, but now resides in northern Virginia with her husband and three children. She was a computer systems manager before she made writing her full-time career. She is a graduate of Virginia State University and holds a bachelor of science in physics.

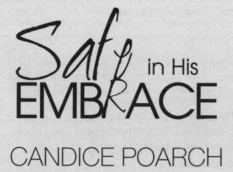

Safe in His
EMBRACE
in His

CANDICE POARCH

KIMANI
ROMANCE

To a dear neighbor, Jim (James) Sorenson,
whose stories of Alaska made me feel as if
I were actually there.
Thank you for being a wonderful neighbor.
You loved wide open spaces and I hope
you are there now in your heart.

 KIMANI PRESS™

PLEASE RECYCLE · THIS PRODUCT IS RECYCLABLE

ISBN-13: 978-0-373-86147-7

Recycling programs
for this product may
not exist in your area.

SAFE IN HIS EMBRACE

www.kimanipress.com

Printed in U.S.A.

Dear Reader,

Thank you for reading *Safe in His Embrace*. I hope you enjoy your travels through the lives of Senetra Blain and Alexander Wilson as they meet in breathtaking Alaska. Follow their passionate journey as they learn to trust and love each other. I hope you enjoy their passion as much as the lovely scenery.

I also hope you have enjoyed each of the Avery women as they have discovered hope and love all the way from Virginia to Alaska. And don't forget George Avery, the grandfather of these three women, who now explores his own new love interest.

Thank you for so many wonderful and inspiring e-mails and letters. You may contact me through my Web site, www.candicepoarch.com, or write to P.O. Box 291, Springfield, VA 22150.

Warmest regards,

Candice Poarch

Chapter 1

Senetra Blain's heart beat erratically as icy points of fear gripped her. She was in her old bedroom in her mother's L.A. home, hastily tossing her things in a suitcase. The pale green walls contrasted with the slightly darker green-and-white bedspread. Her debate, soccer and softball trophies were lined up on shelves. Her ballet costume graced the wall like a beloved portrait. No shelter here. Would she ever see this room again? Would she ever see her mother again? Her stomach clenched. She was running on adrenaline, trying to stay alive one day at a time.

"I don't know how Timothy keeps finding me," she said of her husband. "I just can't get away from him."

"It's entirely my fault," her mother, Dorothelia

Jackson, said. Just looking at Senetra distressed her. Still slightly swollen and bruised, the marks from the assault just now fading to a light purple shade. It would take weeks for the marks to fade completely. Her mother balled her hands into fists, her nails biting into her skin. "I just needed to see you, and look at what he did to you. I'm so sorry."

"Don't you dare take responsibility for Timothy's actions. It wasn't your fault. You didn't do this. He did." Senetra hugged her mother briefly, holding back tears of rage and pain.

Wanting to free herself from Timothy as quickly as possible, Senetra had returned to Milwaukee to sign the divorce papers. Apparently, her husband had been trailing her because he abducted her right off the street. Her sixty-five-year-old mother was knocked to the sidewalk when she tried to stop him.

Timothy took Senetra to the posh home she and he had shared for more than a year. And there he beat her before her mother and her lawyer came tearing in with the police. Senetra didn't know any of that at the time. She'd lost consciousness.

Senetra shook her head and grimaced when pain stabbed her. She'd spent a week in the hospital. She was released yesterday and with security guards her mother had hired, had flown to L.A. with her mother hovering close by.

She was leaving within moments—maybe forever.

Senetra fought tears. "I want to see you, too, Mama. We shouldn't have to stay apart. I shouldn't have to hide. He breaks the law and he gets away with it." Damn it, where was the justice in that? Absurdly, Timothy had claimed self-defense. He had a top-notch attorney to represent him, and so far no charge seemed to stick.

Timothy had started hitting her within six months of their marriage. Senetra refused to take it. She moved out, but she quickly discovered leaving him wasn't so easy. He found her—and of course he beat her. But it was nothing like this time. She knew he'd kill her if he ever found her again.

"There is an option we haven't considered," her mother said.

"Oh?"

"The sperm donor your father and I used to conceive made arrangements for you to contact him if you wanted to," she said. "Did you ever tell Timothy about him?"

"Are you kidding? I had to be from the right pedigree to satisfy his snobbish family."

"They have nothing to turn their noses up at. Your donor father comes from a well-respected family, as do your father and I. Why don't you contact him, honey? If you're in trouble, I'm sure he'll want to help you."

"That's pretty far-fetched, Mama, for me to come out of the blue and announce that I'm his long lost daughter and that I need sanctuary." Senetra zipped up the suitcase.

"Why not? He was a compassionate man. He knew how desperately your father and I wanted you, which was the reason he agreed to the procedure."

"I'll be okay, Mama. I'm more worried about you. I'll find a way to contact you so you'll at least know I'm safe."

"Take this anyway." Dorothelia thrust a small envelope into her hand and Senetra quickly stashed it in her purse. "Will this nightmare ever end?" She took her daughter's face in both hands. "I love you so much. And I miss you. We were so close."

"We still are. He can't change that. We just can't be physically close," she murmured past the lump in her throat. "I'll miss you, Mama. More than you'll ever know."

"I wish your father was still alive."

Her father had died while her mother was pregnant with Senetra. But as he was dying he wrote several small books for her that she cherished dearly. Thank God, she'd left most of them in her mother's home when she married. Otherwise Timothy would have destroyed all of them or held them hostage the way he was holding the two she'd left in Milwaukee. He'd already destroyed one of them.

She hugged her mother tightly and quickly. One of the security guards came for her luggage and reminded them it was time for Senetra to leave. With teary goodbyes she headed for the stairs.

"Maybe...maybe I can join you one day," her mother called after her desperately.

"I'd love that."

"God will find a way so that we can be together."

Senetra would never forget her mother's beautiful, anguished face. Her complexion was a little lighter than Senetra's medium brown. Her hair was curled under and brushed her shoulders. She was an intelligent woman with aristocratic features. Before Senetra's marriage, she'd looked years younger, as if she were in her fifties instead of her sixties. Now she looked her age.

Hours later, Senetra boarded a ship and was on her way to the first leg of her journey. Her mother didn't have a clue as to her destination. She'd worked it out in her mind while she was in the hospital. Alaska was the only place her husband would never think to search.

She and the security guys had set up an elaborate escape. They only knew part of her route. She'd changed her appearance. She wore a wig and colored contacts and dressed twenty pounds heavier than her actual weight.

In the interim she would stay with the sister of a long-ago acquaintance on an island near Seattle to wait to see if he was able to secure a teaching position for her under the new identity the Milwaukee courts had established for her. She'd considered moving to a small, isolated town of no more than three hundred, but a place like that lacked vital services. There were certain things she wasn't willing to give up—teaching and creature comforts.

Settling back in her seat, she pried open the envelope and retrieved a single sheet of paper. "Mackenzie Avery" was printed in her mother's lovely script, along with his address and phone number. He lived in Virginia. Senetra shoved the paper back in the envelope, stashed it again in her purse and glanced around. Since she first ran away, she was always cognizant of her surroundings.

She couldn't contact Mr. Avery. One of her high school friends was also the product of a sperm donor.

They'd made up elaborate plans for her to meet the man, thinking he would welcome her with open arms. Her friend could barely contain her excitement. Senetra remembered the day vividly. It was nice to meet her, her donor father had said. She'd certainly turned into a nice young lady. But he'd made it clear he didn't consider himself her father.

Chapter 2

Eight months was a moment or an eternity.

"Ms. Novak," a voice called up to Senetra's second-floor apartment, loud enough to wake everyone on that side of the building.

She couldn't believe that boy was yelling to her before five o'clock and on a Saturday morning. She pushed the sliding door open and went out on the balcony.

"Hush, Mark, before you wake everyone."

The lanky six-three senior hadn't quite grown into his height. He stood next to his best friend, Anthony Wright. "Dad's leaving soon," he said impatiently. "You're gonna miss him."

"I'm coming down now," she told him.

"Throw down your keys so I can warm up your car."

Handing her keys over to a seventeen-year-old wasn't something a sane teacher would do. But she'd likely miss the older man if she waited to warm up the car when she went downstairs. The temperature had dipped near zero the night before. She retrieved the key and tossed it down to him.

Senetra had arrived in Homer, Alaska, the beginning of September and began to work immediately. They had given her seniors. At first she thought it was a curse. It turned out to be a blessing. It left her very little time to think. Seniors were a handful and although it was only March, they were bursting with excitement about graduation and college.

Except for one of her favorites, Mark Kirill. He was a bright student, but his father was vehemently against him going to college. Senetra agreed to talk to him. The older man was going fishing that morning and she didn't know when he'd return.

Homer might be warmer than most of Alaska, but it was still cold as heck, she thought as she went outside. Gray exhaust was sputtering from her Jeep.

Mark and Anthony got out. "Mom and Dad argued again last night," Mark said, his face furrowed.

Senetra patted his arm. "I'm sorry."

"Mom put him out of the bedroom."

Senetra brushed a hand across her face. Danya Kirill's wife was a tiny woman. The image of her ordering a man the size of a bear around almost had Senetra bubbling with laugher. But she curtailed it. Clearly Mark was distressed.

"He respects you," Mark said. "Maybe you can get him to see reason."

Senetra stifled a moan. She wished Mark hadn't put too much trust in her abilities to persuade his father. "I can't promise you anything, but I'll do my best."

"I know you'll convince him. I just have to go to Anchorage. Anthony and I are gonna be roommates."

"I have to get to the dock first," she said, getting into the Jeep.

She'd sent letters to Mr. Kirill requesting a conference with him, but once he realized her repeated requests dealt with college forms and not some problem the teenager was having in school, he'd ignored them.

The Jeep wasn't actually warm, but the motor was warm enough to drive. She drove the three blocks to the Spit, a small boat harbor with launching facilities and charter boats. On a warm day she would have walked.

The beauty of the Kachemak Bay spread out before her in a seascape worthy of a painting. Gathering her coat around her, she climbed out of the car. Fishermen were still pulling out to sea. The few boats scattered about were a tiny fraction of the bustling activity when she'd arrived. She perused the pier until she located the boat she was searching for. She gave a sigh of relief. The captain was still there with his brother, but the engine was running.

Senetra jogged down the dock, waving her hand to get Danya Kirill's attention. "Mr. Kirill, Mr. Kirill," she shouted. "May I have a moment with you, please?"

He scowled over the motor's loud roar, indicating he'd heard more than enough from her already.

"What is it now?" he growled with a frown designed to send her fleeing. It reminded her of Mark.

"The deadline is almost here. I need you to complete a few forms so Mark can apply for a scholarship."

"How many times have I told you Mark's not going anywhere? He's going to stay right here and fish with me," he said, pointing toward the deck with a long finger. "We're fishermen, Ms. Novak. Now I've got work to do."

"Mr. Kirill. Please," she entreated. "The form doesn't obligate Mark."

"Don't have time to waste. In the summer I can make enough to support my family the entire year. Now, how many jobs can let a man do that these days?"

Mark wanted to attend college desperately, so she renewed her efforts. "Not many. But you obviously enjoy your work. And most of your runs are made during the summer when Mark will be home from college and available to work with you," she said. "Give him a chance to direct his own future."

"I make a good honest living. And I've raised my family in a good, safe community," he said. "And at least my son is safe here."

She hadn't meant to insult the man. "I know safety is important, but accidents happen at sea, too. As much as you want to hold on, one day you have to let him chart his own course," she said. "He's a responsible young man. What Mark wants is the issue here. If he decides to become a fisherman after he graduates, he can do so. He can even fish *while* he's in college since summer is your main season."

"The issue is will he live long enough to graduate? Can you guarantee that, Ms. Novak?"

"You know I can't. Accidents happen everywhere." She felt as if she were losing the argument. "But there's no guarantee he'll remain safe here, either."

"Viktor's death wasn't an accident. Besides, Mark doesn't know what he wants at his age."

"All I'm asking is for you to give him choices. Complete the forms just in case you change your mind."

His face settled into an ominous scowl and his bushy brows drew together in a thick straight line. "You're wasting my time and yours. I won't change my mind. I've said my last piece on the matter." Ignoring her, he started talking to his brother who offered Senetra a sad smile.

They cast off and the boat moved away from the pier. Mr. Kirill was a big man. Six-three at least, his Russian ancestry prevalent in the full black-and-gray beard springing from his wind-whipped face. But he was solid and he stood on deck wearing a checkered chambray jacket as if the cold didn't penetrate.

Frustrated, Senetra gazed at the stern of the boat until it was a mere fleck on the horizon.

She'd wanted to have a private conversation with him, not screaming on the dock where everyone around could listen in. But the man made it impossible.

She wasn't insulted by the older man's attitude. His

words were laced with pain and sorrow. She understood loss and how hard it was to overcome.

The Kirills had sent Viktor, four years older than Mark, away to college. During his sophomore year, he'd died in a hazing incident while pledging to a fraternity. The family was still reeling from the loss. From what she'd heard, Mark and his brother were polar opposites. Viktor was more outgoing. The popular son who'd engaged in practically every sport. He'd lived the life of a high school and college star. The girls hung on his arms like barnacles on ships.

Senetra understood Mr. Kirill's reluctance to send another child out into the world. But Mark was his own person and shouldn't be held accountable for his brother's mistakes.

Crossing her arms, she stared across the bay at the mountains until the penetrating cold prompted her to seek warmth.

Some positive effect she'd had. What a joke. She'd had no impact whatsoever, except frustrating the man further. She'd regroup and think of another strategy. She had to find a way to reach him. She wasn't giving up.

The piercing cold had Senetra hovering in her jacket. Alaska was a place she'd always wanted to visit, but never dreamed of living in. Most of the time she'd been there, it had been cold—not the cold of Nome or even twenty miles north, but an entirely different world from L.A. The early March wind here was like a cold hand constantly slapping at her, but no worse than a windy day in Wisconsin, she thought as she drove one block to the restaurant where she was meeting her friend.

It was bustling with activity. Today was Senetra's twenty-seventh birthday. There had been a time when she'd wondered if she'd make it.

At times like this she missed her mother and her old friends. She was Regina Novak now. Ah, no sense in dwelling in the past. Couldn't do a thing about it.

A friend and fellow teacher, Kathryn Rimes, was meeting her at six for a birthday breakfast. Why she'd want to meet at such an ungodly hour was beyond reasoning.

They were going to look at huskies after breakfast. Senetra wanted a dog to cuddle up with in front of the fire. Huskies were trusting. They treated you well. Not like men, who'd worry you and whose tempers you could never predict. She still startled at noises in the night. This summer she'd have time to train a dog. But today she was just going to look.

Senetra picked up the Anchorage and local newspapers and the waitress led her to a corner table.

"Just coffee for now," Senetra murmured. "I'm waiting for someone." When the woman left, Senetra opened the newspaper and began to read, but she wasn't alone long. Several of her students and their parents stopped by, as well as several of her new friends.

Even Charles Palmer, her karate teacher, gave her a pained greeting. Poor man. Senetra hadn't kicked him intentionally in Thursday's class. She simply wasn't very adept at karate.

A month ago, she'd decided it was time she got off

her butt and moved forward with her life. She was tired of looking around corners, waiting for Timothy to accost her.

She was determined to live her life as if he'd never find her. But she wasn't a fool. She needed protection and the best protection was to be able to protect herself physically.

She was the newest student in Charles's class. She knew he hoped she'd drop out. He'd even offered to reimburse her if she decided the class wasn't for her. After she kicked him in the thigh Thursday, he'd renewed his offer. But she told him not to fear. She was going to stick it out to the bitter end. He'd grunted as he limped away.

The week before, she'd missed his groin by an inch. But she was determined to learn. Senetra shook her head. She'd thought karate instructors were adept at dodging mishaps.

Even the kids made fun of her poor skills and lack of coordination.

One thing was certain, they could learn from her persistence. Anything worth learning was worth sticking to, even in difficult times.

She beckoned to Charles.

With coffee in hand, he limped forward with the enthusiasm of approaching a guillotine. His gray hair indicated late fifties, but you could never tell. Some people didn't age well. He'd combed his hair to cover a bald spot. Since his cap had disturbed the arrangement, his white scalp shone through.

"Ms. Novak. A fine morning," he said through pinched lips, clutching his hand around his cup.

"I wanted to discuss a proposition with you," Senetra said, gesturing to a seat. Sensing his hesitation, she said, "I won't take long."

The man paled even further as he slowly lowered himself into the farthest chair from her, but Senetra didn't take offense.

"Spring is right around the corner and I'm sure some of the women in the women's center would love to take your course. I'll even be willing to talk to the center's manager and some of the women or help make broch—"

Senetra stopped when Charles choked on his coffee. He grabbed a napkin and dabbed at his lips.

"Are you all right, Mr. Palmer? Can I get you a glass of water or something?" she asked. Beckoning a passing waitress, she started to get up to thump him on the back. "Is the coffee too hot?"

Eyes watering, Charles raised his hand, vigorously waving her back to her seat.

"Fine...fine," he choked out. "The coffee's fine. Thank you for your offer, but unfortunately, I'll be leaving at the beginning of the summer. I'm sure the next teacher will be grateful for your assistance."

"Oh," Senetra muttered, disappointed. "Where are you going?"

"I'm not sure yet. I've been given two offers and I have a month to make a decision."

Frowning with disappointment, Senetra said, "We'll

be sorry to see you go. Is your daughter leaving, too?"

"She hasn't decided, but I'm moving because of a family emergency." He stood and looked toward the door. "Ah, here's my daughter now."

Senetra glanced in that direction. Sure enough, Laura Palmer was standing at the entrance talking to someone and waving her fingers. "She just got engaged."

"Congratulations," Senetra said. "Grant's a really nice guy. You must be pleased."

"Yes, I am."

Senetra sighed wistfully. "She's going to miss you when you leave. I hope things work out well with you and your family." But at least his daughter and he could communicate. He'd know where his daughter was and could pick up the phone anytime and call her, which wasn't the case for Senetra and her mother.

"Some things can't be helped. Have a good morning," he muttered, and began to move away.

"I'll see you at Tuesday's class," Senetra reminded him, as if he needed it.

Senetra wasn't sure, but it sounded as if he muttered "Unfortunately," as he hurriedly limped away.

Laura Palmer dated Grant. He and his older brother owned the Pit, a popular bar near the dock. Grant was forever breaking up fights and getting injuries for his trouble. But he was one of the nicest guys she'd met and Laura was a lucky woman to have him. When Senetra was ready to date again, she could see herself dating someone with Grant's temperament, not that she was thinking along those lines. It was way too soon.

Chapter 3

Alexander Wilson's dad often forgot the time difference between Wisconsin and Alaska and because he'd farmed his entire life he was accustomed to early-morning hours. However, it often presented a problem for Alex, especially when he took the rare opportunity to sleep in. When the phone rang at five that Saturday morning, Alex dragged his hand from beneath the covers to pick up the receiver, knowing the identity of the caller without glancing at the phone's display. But he wouldn't complain. He'd almost lost the older man a couple of years back.

"Morning, Dad." He turned over in the bed.

"Son, I didn't want to call you so early, but I thought

you should know before someone else told you." His father's voice was regretful and hesitant.

Alex sat up in bed. There was no question who his father was talking about. All his conversations about Jessica Potts started out the same way. "What is it?"

"I wish you had gone on and married that girl," his father said for what had to be the thousandth time. "You know I'm at the end of my days. Yours is just beginning. I married the love of my life and our life was great together. I wanted the same for you—for all my children."

"Dad, your life isn't over. You've got plenty to live for. Things weren't always perfect with Jessica and me, you know."

"It's never perfect. You're two different people, but you have the same basic values, believe in the same things. You loved each other, and that's the most important thing. The life you could have built together would have been a great one."

"If Jessica and I were meant to marry, we would have." Easy words, but pain still grabbed Alex's chest just thinking about Jessica being married to another man. She hadn't waited more than six months after he'd left Wisconsin to move on. He'd asked her not to wait for him, but he thought she'd wait anyway. He'd thought that she'd loved him that much. After all, she knew the reason he'd accepted a job in Alaska. And she knew it was temporary.

"She's pregnant."

Alex wasn't prepared for this. Not at all. For moments he didn't respond. He should have been prepared. She was married, had moved on long ago. Alex shook his head to clear it, but it was useless.

"She was supposed to be your—"

"No, she wasn't." Alex cleared his throat and swallowed hard as if it would change anything. "You're going to send your blood pressure up worrying about that. We're still good friends, Dad. Will always be friends. I saw her in church the last time I was home," he said. "Just think about it. Would she have married another man if she was really in love with me?" Alex was saying this more for himself than for his dad. But he couldn't stop the… He didn't know what he felt. Did he still love Jessica? Had their love been the love of a lifetime? Was there such a thing as the connection his parents had had?

Worst of all, was the sorrow he felt for losing Jessica or was it for the loss of a dream? He'd wanted a love like the one his mom and dad had experienced. He knew his father would never again find a love like what he'd felt for his late wife. And her love for him had been equally powerful.

Raymond sighed. "Women get tired of waiting, son. And it's been a while since you saw her."

"You're talking like I'm an old man. I'm in the prime of my life." Was it too much to expect a woman to wait two years? What were two years in the scheme of life? Alex was twenty-nine. He tried to tell himself if Jessica could give up on him this quickly, their relationship wouldn't have survived the hard times.

Maybe he was at fault. Perhaps if he'd asked her to

wait, she would have. It was too late for what-ifs. Since he didn't ask her, he'd never know.

"Life doesn't sit still for anyone. Come home, son. It's time."

"In a couple of years. And I'm coming to visit you this summer for a week, not the usual day or two. Who knows, I might have someone with me." This again was for his father's benefit. He didn't believe for a moment he'd find anyone.

"Jessica is a good woman."

Alex heard the sadness in his father's voice. He'd liked Jessica.

"I've messed up your whole life. It's just after your mother got so sick, I let some things go that I shouldn't have. But she used to take care of the insurance and farm paperwork."

"Stop blaming yourself." It saddened him to hear his father talk this way. He'd been a hardworking man his entire life—worked from sunup to sundown until the accident. He and Alex's mother paid for college educations for all their children. They'd even brought Alex, their youngest, a car while his sisters and brothers had shared family cars.

"I've never regretted being able to do something for you for a change. Not ever. You've done a lot for me—for all of us. And I've moved on. It's time you do, too."

Alex wanted to forget Jessica existed. He swiped a hand across his face. "So, tell me, how are you?"

"Doing great. Finished with the therapy."

"That's good, really good."

"Do they have some nice young women where you are?" His father's voice had a desperate appeal.

"Some, but don't worry about that. Take care, Dad." Alex hung up. Placing his hands behind his head, he stared at the ceiling.

He had been a day from asking Jessica to marry him when his father was injured. The tractor had tipped over and trapped him while he was working. It took several surgeries and months of rehab to get him walking again, and even longer to get him to where he was. But he was walking without a cane. If Alex had to do it all over again, he'd make the same decision without a thought.

His father's insurance had expired a year before the accident, but none of the children knew that. Somehow he got the idea that his parents would live forever. But his dad wasn't old enough for Medicare, so he would have had to sell the farm to pay for the surgeries and therapy.

All of Alex's siblings were married and most of them had children, some almost ready for college. Alex was single and no one depended on him. A friend of his worked for Arctic Oil and had asked him to work with him. He'd always declined. Jessica couldn't move with him and wouldn't move there even if she could. But the pay was way above average. It took him less than two years to pay off his father's medical bills.

He'd made the last payment a couple of months ago. Now that his dad was old enough for Medicare to kick in, supplemental insurance was easier to get. But now Alex was building a cushion. The one thing the accident

had taught him was to be prepared for the unex-
pected.

Alex glared at the ceiling. Jessica was married—and
pregnant—and he had no one to rush home to
anyway.

No sense in lying in bed. He climbed out, showered
and dressed for the day. He packed his overnight bag
and added a couple of energy bars. He was on leave for
a week. His friend, Rick Cardwell, had invited him to
a birthday celebration for the weekend starting with
breakfast. They had been roommates in college. Alex
shook his head. It seemed like a lifetime ago. The two
of them were going to take off for some fishing
afterward.

Alex chuckled. His father wanted him to find a
woman in the least likely place on earth—where the
men outnumbered women by a wide margin.

He made his way to the restaurant and glanced
around for Rick—and did a double take. It couldn't be.
At the bar, he spotted a gorgeous sister with dark brown
hair sitting in a corner reading a paper. Last summer
when he'd visited, he saw a couple of black men, but no
black women. He considered joining her, but decided
against it. She was probably married or with a boyfriend.
But he couldn't stop himself from gazing at her from
the corner of his eye.

On second thought, what was he saving himself for?
This was the first complete week off in two years.

Her head turned as she listened and smiled at
someone. At that angle, Alex recognized something

familiar about the way she moved. But he was certain this was his first encounter with her.

Fifteen minutes later, Kathryn Rimes hustled in the front door, her windblown hair gathered into a blond ponytail. She looked startled to see Senetra.

"Honey, you're not in a rush, are you?" she called out, approaching Senetra's table. She was a couple of inches taller than Senetra's five-five. They taught next door to each other, Kathryn history and Senetra math, and they lived in the same apartment building.

"I was already out and decided to nurse a cup of coffee until you arrived."

"I have to meet someone in the other room. Back in a sec."

Senetra waved her on.

Twenty minutes later and another cupful of coffee, Senetra was feeling jittery and her stomach was growling from the aroma of food when Kathryn made another appearance. "We're going to the room in back where it's quieter so we can hear ourselves talk," she said.

"Sure." Senetra wondered why this table in the quiet corner wouldn't suffice. It was busy, but not that busy. She closed the paper.

"Just leave it on the table."

After leaving a tip, Senetra followed Kathryn, but the room they approached was far more crowded than the one they'd left.

"Happy birthday!" everyone shouted. There were at least a hundred people.

It took a moment for Senetra to take it all in. They

were here for her birthday? She was a newcomer. Her heart swelled and tears glistened in her eyes. She just couldn't believe it.

Iris Kirill stood front and center. Mark and Anthony were seated at a huge table with other teens. Iris was somewhere between forty and forty-five and stood no taller than five-three, but she could command a place like the captain of a fleet. She was also the head of the quilting bee, and she was Danya Kirill's wife. She was one of those sturdy women who were always in perpetual motion. Her chestnut hair was cut to brush her shoulders.

Kathryn looped an arm around Senetra's shoulder, squeezed briefly and gathered a plate from the buffet where a huge breakfast was spread out.

"You guys." Senetra swiped the tears from her eyes.

"You don't have time for tears," Iris said. "Eat up. We've got a million things scheduled."

Senetra wondered what those million things consisted of, but didn't have time to dwell on it. Kathryn handed her a stack of pancakes with seven candles. "Make a wish," she said quietly.

Senetra closed her eyes briefly, made her wish and blew out the candles. There wasn't even a remote chance of her wish coming true, to be able to live in peace, free of her husband's harassment, but she wished for it anyway.

She gazed at the happy faces surrounding her. None of her friends knew of her background. Not even Kathryn. None of them really knew *her,* yet they'd accepted her into their circle. They refused to leave her to her own devices and to live on the fringe as she'd planned.

Determined not to let Timothy intrude on her wonderful surprise, she swatted his presence from her mind the way one would a pesky fly.

After a rough hug, Iris guided her to the head of the line. Like well-ordered soldiers, everyone fell in line behind Senetra.

With difficulty Senetra brought her emotions under control and wiped new tears from her eyes with a napkin. Her plan had been to spend the weekend alone. She glanced at the smiling faces around her. This was their day off. Most had children they could spend the time with. It was a wonderful thing that whatever trouble life dished up, there was always kindness waiting to befriend you, even strangers.

Once seated at a table with Kathryn and Iris, she noticed a handsome man at the table with Rick. He was new in town. Apprehension skittered along her spine.

"Ms. Novak." Joseph, a retired fisherman who made runs with Danya when he wanted to make extra money, jerked her attention away from the newcomer. Joe's plate was heaping with enough food to feed three people. He appeared to be in his eighties and his cologne was so strong Senetra's eyes watered as she stifled a cough. He'd even added a bow tie to his chambray shirt. "May I have the first dance?"

"This is a breakfast, Joe, not a dance," Iris said. "What in heaven's name did you douse yourself with?" She fanned as if she could wave the scent away.

"I got all dressed up and used my favorite cologne," he said.

"I'm deeply touched," Senetra said. "Thank you for helping me celebrate my birthday."

"What a shame we can't dance," he said, and went in search of a table.

Senetra forgot the newcomer as she began to socialize with others at her table.

After breakfast everyone scattered except Kathryn and her boyfriend, Rick, a high school science teacher, and the man Senetra spotted earlier. He said something to Rick before he left.

"Well, time to pack an overnight bag," Kathryn said, looking sheepish. "Shouldn't take but a few minutes. You did do laundry last night, didn't you?"

Senetra tensed and frowned. "Where am I going?" she asked suspiciously.

"It's a surprise, but pack warm and comfortable clothing. We'll return late tomorrow," Kathryn said. "We thought about sending you alone, but I know you'd never go if we didn't drag you kicking and screaming. You're the only one I've met who won't go sightseeing and there're so many places to explore here."

Senetra's gut tightened. "Now I'm really curious."

"It's a surprise," Rick repeated, glancing at his watch, clearly impatient to be on his way.

"Relax," Kathryn scolded, smoothing her tense hands. "We aren't going far. Listen, everyone chipped in. They want to give you a special gift for your birthday."

"You traitor," Senetra said without heat. "I thought I asked you not to tell anyone."

"I couldn't do that. Your neighbors love you. So do your students. They would have felt betrayed if I'd kept silent." She smiled. "Don't forget to pack your bikini."

"Bikini?" Senetra teased. "Sounds like Hawaii."

"Wish we could be so lucky," she said. "No planes. Just a short ferry ride."

Senetra recalled the smiling faces of the people who'd just filed out. The ones who'd gotten up early on Saturday morning to wish her a cheerful, special day.

She hugged Kathryn. "Thank you."

So much for her trip to the kennel to look over cute little huskies, she thought, but relaxed somewhat.

Rick loved the out-of-doors and, knowing him, he'd have them stashed away in some remote fishing cabin where they were the only inhabitants for forty miles. She hoped they had running water and a flushing toilet, at least. Still, she hated when she wasn't in control, hated being any place where she hadn't mapped out an escape route. She was fortunate to have escaped Timothy the last time and she knew if he found her again, she wasn't going to be so lucky.

She sighed. Fear wasn't going to ruin her birthday celebration.

Alex stood by himself on the ferry, waiting for Rick.

"I'm telling you, the teacher's a looker," Bob Taylor,

the ferry captain, declared. "She teaches my sister's boy and the kid's fallen head over heels in love with her."

Alex already knew that. Lots of students were present at the breakfast. "This isn't a date, Bob." Rick had told him they were going to some remote place overnight. He hadn't mentioned setting him up with anyone.

"You could make it into one, all tucked up and cozy at the B and B. Good for a man to have a woman on his arm when bitter winter settles in. Better than a bottle of Jack Daniel's any day." He elbowed Alex and winked. "Oyster's their specialty."

Alex couldn't help grinning at the man's foolishness. "Spring's right around the corner," he said. "How many women have you tried to set me up with? I just got here yesterday." Alex often rode Bob's ferry whenever he visited Homer. And every trip the older man tried to fix him up with a date.

"Not that many single ones around," Bob murmured. "You better get her before someone snatches her up. I'm surprised she's still unattached. You're gonna have your work cut out for you."

Laughing, Alex tossed his duffel bag on the floor and fished out his wallet to pay for his ticket. The first thing he saw was a ragged-edged photo of Jessica and him. He slipped it back in. When he returned from his trip, he was going to pack it away. He had no business dreaming about her.

At this very moment, he imagined her giddy and happy, surrounded by family and friends celebrating her good news.

Alex shook his head. He couldn't go on like this. Bob

believed it wasn't good for men to be alone, but right now he needed to be alone. Despite what he'd told his father, he had a long way to go before he completely got over Jessica.

Senetra sat in the backseat. Rick drove the couple of blocks to the Spit as if driving for NASCAR. After all the wheedling and cajoling, Senetra still didn't know their destination.

"I hope you don't get seasick," Rick said. She could hear the eagerness in his voice.

"A fine time to ask her," Kathryn muttered, turning around in the seat. "You *don't* get seasick, do you? I brought something along just in case."

"I have a cast-iron stomach." Just a small exaggeration since at that very moment her insides were fluttering like Jell-O.

Rick drove onto the ferry and slid his SUV into a tight space. They all climbed out. The ferry was going south, making many stops along the way. They could be debarking anywhere between Homer and Kodiak.

Kathryn waved to someone. "There's Alex. We have a few minutes to spare."

Senetra finally spotted a man talking to the captain—the stranger at the party. Thick, black eyelashes, handsome face, medium brown complexion. Hair slightly curly. He wore a thick sheepskin jacket over jeans. God, he was handsome. Her insides quivered with awareness. Even his smile was sexy. She was amazed at her attraction to him. She thought Timothy had killed that part of her for at least a decade. His gaze touched hers briefly.

"He's not going with us, is he?" she whispered to Kathryn.

"Of course he is."

"I'm going to kill you," Senetra gritted between clenched teeth.

"Relax. He's Rick's friend and he doesn't take vacations often, so when he told Rick he was coming to town, Rick invited him along. What else could he do? You can't deny the guy a vacation, can you?"

"How convenient."

Kathryn humored her with a huge grin. This was a setup she couldn't get out of. Senetra quietly studied the very handsome man with skin tone just a little darker than her own.

"Hello," Alex called out, and a cold chill raced up Senetra's spine. Strangers made her uncomfortable. This was one of the reasons she hadn't visited the heavily touristy sites.

Even so, she knew all too well the world was very small. But it was just a weekend, not the rest of her life. That's what she'd told herself eight months ago when she'd gone home to sign the divorce papers. She'd disguised herself, but it didn't work.

Senetra closed her eyes briefly. *Don't let Timothy spoil your birthday. He's already spoiled enough in your life. This man knows nothing about Timothy or the old Senetra.* As far as he knew, she was Regina Novak, the new teacher in town.

"Let me store your bag in the car," Rick said.

"Sure," Alex murmured, but his eyes caressed Senetra and she was shocked at how a sparkle of desire flashed through her, caressing her skin with hot licks of flame. She hadn't felt desire like this for years and she felt fear of another kind entirely.

"Alex, meet Regina Novak. This is Alex Wilson, a friend of mine. He's on a week's vacation from Valdez," Rick said as if this were a blind date. "And he's ready for a good time."

Senetra wasn't anybody's good time, but she politely extended her hand to accept his handshake. "Hello, Alex." His touch was firm, and she kept her expression neutral. She didn't want him getting any ideas that she was going to be his weekend R & R.

Alex's smile was cautious. "A pleasure to meet you."

Senetra read his "not interested" signal loud and clear and that was fine by her. But there was something familiar about him, and her apprehension came back full force. She didn't recognize his name. As a teacher, and having to know all the right people for Timothy's political career, she remembered names and faces, but couldn't recall ever being introduced to Alex. So why did his face seem so familiar?

Senetra shook her head. This wasn't the first time she'd wondered if a face was familiar. Through Timothy's political connections, she'd met thousands of people, but knew few of them.

Senetra walked to the railing with Kathryn. Moments later Alex and Rick joined them and surreptitiously she glanced at Alex again. She didn't know him and he didn't know her. She renewed her promise to be aware, but to enjoy her birthday weekend.

Alex's stomach clenched in recognition and the same desire that stole his breath. He knew her, not as Regina Novak, but as Senetra Blain—Mrs. Timothy Blain. It was three years ago at a fund-raiser when he first spotted her standing alone across the room. His cousin had an argument with his girlfriend and had an extra ticket, and since he was in town, invited Alex to go.

Senetra wore a stunning gown that fit her voluptuous figure to perfection. A figure she displayed with tasteful abandon. With a desire unlike anything he'd experienced before, Alex had wanted to run his hands slowly all over her delectable body.

Her hair was fashioned in a sophisticated style that exposed her neck. He'd wanted to release the pins and rake his hand through the silky strands while he kissed every inch of her neck. That was before he saw that she dripped with diamonds.

Even knowing she was way out of his league, he couldn't help himself. As if mesmerized, he'd started across the room for an introduction. But when he was three yards away, he'd stopped. A man joined her and Alex spotted her diamond-studded wedding band and the huge three-or-four-carat diamond engagement ring with it and backed up a step.

The man linked her hand in the crook of his arm and the couple strolled away. Alex made his way to the open bar, where he caught up with his cousin.

"Tell me about Mrs. Blain," he said.

"There's very little talk, only that she's Timothy Blain's wife and he's very possessive. She teaches at some high school, but he's not too thrilled about that."

Alex shook his head. His heart pounded. His mouth went dry. She was no more than five-five or six. She licked her full lips, drawing his gaze. Her high cheekbones reddened as the wind whipped against her skin. Even without the glitter she was stunning. But the *M-R-S* definitely put her on the unavailable list.

He wondered again why Mrs. Timothy Blain was in Alaska without all her glitter—without the rings. He stood a few feet from her, allowing himself one quick glimpse. Even without the makeup and shortened hair, she was damn sexy.

And his body responded to her every bit as explosively as it had three years ago. This was going to be one hell of a weekend.

"Didn't I say she was a beauty?" Rick whispered.

"And didn't I say I wasn't looking?"

"Hell, man, you're always looking, whether you admit it or not. Besides, you can't moon over Jessica for the rest of your life."

"Since we're getting personal, why don't you ask Kathryn to marry you?"

"This is about you and Regina. Not me."

Great, his friend was trying to hook him up with a married woman when he was trying to get over another married woman. He didn't need this crap.

Timothy Blain worked hard at his job. He was well respected in Milwaukee and the brains behind the mayor's election.

Mrs. Blain was a hothouse flower. He could imagine Timothy not having enough time to entertain her. Did she leave to teach him a lesson for ignoring her the way Jessica had taught him a lesson for leaving her? Senetra was at least ten years younger than her husband. Women did devious things to grab attention.

Back home she had everything—money, prestige. Why was she hiding? No doubt, she'd eventually go back to the glamour of her life in Milwaukee. He couldn't imagine her being satisfied here for very long.

After this weekend he was never going to see her again.

He glanced at her again and caught her watching him. He felt drawn again, damn it. Then as now, he wanted to approach her, touch her soft skin. He shook his head. How could a chance moment have such a lasting effect? Their gazes met for several seconds before he tore his attention away to appreciate the beauty of the area. But although nature's beauty intrigued and soothed him, he was deeply disturbed by the woman who stood much too close.

They zipped across the bay, enjoying the backdrop of the magnificent Kenai Mountains, which protected the town from the worst of winter weather, but hid the sun most of the winter.

"We're staying in a quaint B and B near Kenai National Park," Kathryn said. "You're going to love it."

"I know Rick will," Senetra said, lifting her face to the breeze.

Kathryn laughed. "You'd think it was *his* birthday the way he's carrying on. He could barely wait for breakfast to be over. You saw the fishing rods in back, didn't you?"

"Are we really going fishing before daybreak?" Senetra asked with trepidation. The last thing she wanted to do was stand out in the early morning cold holding a fishing pole. When her gaze had collided with Alex's, he'd completely unnerved her.

"I know I'm not. If you want to, feel free to do so while I jump in the hot tub and read a book."

"The hot tub sounds heavenly, but unfortunately I forgot to pack a book."

"I bought extra," Kathryn assured her. "In case you're interested, Rick and Alex were roommates in college."

"Who said I'm interested?" she asked, although she was pleased Kathryn offered the information. She didn't ask questions about others because she was unwilling to divulge her history.

"Oh, God. There it is. Have you ever seen anything so spectacular?" Kathryn said in awe.

Senetra gazed below at blue crystal ice fields that seemed to sprout up from the water. Ninety percent of it was beneath the water's surface, but the part above was breathtaking enough. What beauty.

"We're going to walk on the glacier. You'll love it."

Senetra glanced around apprehensively. "Will many people be at the B and B?"

"Not this time of year. We'll practically have the place to ourselves."

Senetra relaxed somewhat, but she couldn't wipe out the sense of familiarity she felt about Alex. She shook her head.

A lot of special people had gone to expense and trouble to plan a wonderful birthday celebration for her, and she was worried about Timothy.

She stopped mentally beating herself. She couldn't forget the object of this game was to stay alive. And to do that she had to be aware. Awareness was the operative word, not paranoia.

She forced herself to relax and enjoy the view.

His friends had done a fine job, Alex thought. His room was not only next door to Senetra's; it had an attached door they had only to open on both sides if they chose. Rick and Kathryn shared a room across the hall.

He set his duffel bag on the chair and unpacked his gear. They were meeting in a few minutes.

Alex shook his head. Rick and Kathryn couldn't have been more blatant about their matchmaking attempts. He made his way to the lobby. They were heading to the glacier.

Truth be told, Senetra didn't exactly offer herself as if she was in the market. He'd better get used to her being called Regina before he slipped up.

Chapter 4

The sun shone brightly as they walked on the glacier, ice crunching beneath their feet. Of necessity Alex and Senetra walked side by side, while Rick led the way with Kathryn. As much as Alex wanted to feel nothing for Senetra, he was very aware of her presence. He enjoyed her awestruck expression as she was taken to another world by the craggy surface of the glacier.

"First time?" he asked.

"Yes," she said with a smile, and he wondered why she hadn't ventured out more. It was a short water taxi ride from her home.

"Have you been here before?" she asked.

"A couple of times. I've seen other glaciers and ice fields."

"Was it anything like this?" There was something refreshing in observing a person encountering something new in nature.

He nodded. "But there's nothing like your first experience."

"No," she said softly. Their eyes met and touched and for a moment they were in accord. He saw the gorgeous woman whom he wanted to know better and who pulled him across the space of a room.

Up ahead, Rick scouted out places to slide. Kathryn was certain he was going to slide right off the glacier and into the frigid bay and get lost forever in the shards of broken ice.

He merely glided right past her, laughing as he did, then feigned a slip that became very real when he fell on his backside and slid a few feet.

"Will you listen to me now?" Kathryn exploded, her face red with concern and the cold.

"Where's the fun in that?" Rick asked, grinning as he got to his feet and dusted off his backside. Kathryn huffed out a long, frustrated breath.

"Being Rick's roommate must have been interesting," Senetra said around a chuckle.

Alex smiled. "Very." She didn't know the half of it. To his father's disapproval, Rick had taken him mountain climbing the summer of their sophomore year, not to mention caving. There were other exploits over the years and as he looked back, Alex always managed to have a great time.

Senetra rubbed her hands together. On an impulse Alex took them between his own and rubbed them.

"Warmer?" he asked, the condensation from his breath making a cloud.

Warmer? It was a wonder the ice wasn't melting around her. Senetra nodded, heat exploding through her as if he'd zapped her with an electrical charge.

This was ridiculous, she thought, sliding her hands away. Absolutely ridiculous. There was no way she should feel anything for this stranger, much less this intense desire. She'd only met him that morning.

Senetra sighed and gazed at the glacier again. It had rained recently, washing some of the dirt off the blue-white surface. If only the baggage of her life could be wiped away as easily. If only she could do anything without thinking of Timothy.

After another half hour in the area, they gathered oysters from the farm and shucked them. While the chef prepared their dinner, they snowshoed through the forest with Rick leading the way.

Later, they ate an exquisite oyster dinner, sharing two bottles of wine over lively conversation. Afterward, everyone was feeling mellow and Alex was looking even better.

Senetra needed to escape.

When they were on their way to their rooms, Senetra realized she was enjoying herself, that for a space in time she forgot to be apprehensive of Alex.

When Kathryn and Rick went for a dip in the hot tub, she declined to join them, giving the lovebirds their privacy. In her room she wrote a letter to her mother about her birthday weekend, leaving out any details that might give away her location.

At eleven, she still wasn't sleepy. She donned her bathing suit and terry cloth robe.

The hot tub should be empty, she thought as she made her way outside on the crisp night. The hot water would warm her up quickly. That and the glass of wine she'd saved. Her back was turned to the tub as she closed the sliding door.

"Be careful you don't spill it."

Senetra barely stifled a shriek and swiveled around. Whom did she see but Alex? "Sorry, I thought everyone had turned in. I didn't mean to intrude." She started back through the door.

"It's large enough for both of us. I don't bite," he said. His eyes were half-closed.

Senetra's gaze left his attractive face and traveled downward. His bare chest was exposed to her view, all gorgeous muscles and sprinkling of hair.

Common sense told her to go back inside to bed and sleep it off. It was too intimate with just the two of them, but she would seem ridiculous if she left, as if she was running. Shrugging off the robe, she quickly stepped into the steamy water and ducked under the surface until it foamed around her neck. The contrast between the hot water and the cold surroundings was comforting, but she was too unnerved to enjoy the sensation.

"Ahh, this is wonderful," Alex said, closing his eyes and leaning back.

For several moments they were enveloped in uncomfortable silence. Then suddenly he said, "There it is."

"What?"

"Look up."

She turned until she saw it, too. The aurora borealis. No matter the shape or what hues the waving lights took, it was a breathtaking display across the night sky. As Senetra watched the show and felt the texture of the swirling water, the tension slowly ebbed from her.

"So what brought you to Alaska?" Alex asked.

Senetra shrugged, and stiffened. *Stay as close to the truth as possible.* "I've always wanted to visit and to live in a small town. This suits me. It's different from the lower forty-eight. The pace is less frantic. What brought you here?"

"Arctic Oil."

"What do you do for them?"

"I'm a chemical engineer."

"You should talk to my class before you leave."

He chuckled. "Believe me, Rick has roped me every year since I've been here."

Senetra smiled. "Rick knows everyone. He's always getting some professional to speak to the students. So you've made Alaska your home?"

"I'll be here another two to three years before I return to Wisconsin."

Senetra tensed again. This was too much of a co-incidence, although Wisconsin was a large state. "What part?"

"Near Madison."

Even worse. Just an hour from Milwaukee.

"Where are you from?" he asked.

"New York." Senetra had repeated it so many times she now said it without conscious thought.

"New York's a large state."

"Buffalo."

"Then the cold here shouldn't bother you," Alex said, still wondering why she was lying. "It might be even warmer here than in Buffalo. How does your family feel about your being so far from home?"

"I don't have any. This is beginning to feel like the Spanish Inquisition."

Alex sipped his wine. "I thought it was conversation designed for us to get to know each other better. Feel free to ask me anything."

"I came out here to relax." She promptly closed her eyes and settled back, effectively ending the conversation and exposing the long column of her soft neck.

Still the diva, Alex thought, as cold as a Fairbanks winter.

Blowing out a breath, he set down his glass. As much as she irritated him, he shouldn't be curious. He shouldn't want to kiss her smooth skin, but he did, or run his hands and lips over her body. His pulse raced, damn it. He grabbed his wine and swallowed deeply. He'd definitely been without a woman too long.

"You're in the wrong position. You shouldn't miss this fantastic play of lights," he said. "The aurora's moved behind you. The object of a hot tub is to relax the muscles, not get a cramp looking over your shoulder." He chuckled. "Rick trusts me and so does Kat. If I was dangerous they wouldn't let you near me. Come on. Slide over here. I'm not Dracula."

The tub wasn't very large and she moved around until her arm touched his. Her arm was soft. She jerked away as if he'd prodded her with a cattle prod. In complete silence, they watched the lights. But Alex was enjoying just being near her. Although he had to remind himself that she was married.

As she watched the play of lights, he studied her closely. The rippling water revealed faint scars on her shoulder.

"Look there," Alex said, pointing upward. "That shape looks like a prom gown. Do you see it?"

Soon, Senetra was also claiming to see ridiculous objects in the night sky. They were soon laughing hard.

Before he could stop himself, he touched a scar, drawing a line on her arm. "What happened?" She jumped as if he'd struck her. "I wouldn't hurt you," he whispered.

"I should go in."

She moved to get up, but he kissed the length of the scar. Her breath hissed and he paused, then resumed his pursuit. He kissed her shoulder, her neck, her cheek. He pulled back and watched her stare at him wide-eyed.

"What are you doing?" she whispered.

"Going out of my mind." When she didn't move away, he leaned forward and kissed her lightly on the lips, expecting her to either jerk away or slap him. One taste of her was worth a little pain.

When she still didn't move, he gathered her in his arms and ran his tongue against the seam of her lips. She opened for him, allowing his first taste of pure bliss.

Dragging her onto his lap, he stroked her tongue with

his, sucking gently. He caressed her slowly. First her arm; then he moved down to her waist and hips. Her sweet moans drove him wild. When he touched her thigh he felt her hands tentatively stroke him in return. A blaze heated his blood so hot he thought he'd burn from pure need. He couldn't get enough of her.

Her skin was so soft, so warm. When he kissed her neck she ran her hands lightly down his arm and neck, pushing him over the brink of sanity. Two years. Two long years since he'd felt this desire—since he'd wanted a woman as desperately as this.

He eased his hand beneath Senetra's swimsuit, stroking her intimately. Senetra gasped from shock and pleasure. She knew the sensible thing was to make him stop, to get up and leave, but sense didn't enter into the equation as he nudged her bathing suit top aside, fixing his lips around her nipple, stroking his tongue back and forth before taking the taut bud gently between his teeth. He stroked the heat of her desire, stoking a fire so hot she came unglued. It had been so long. So long. In the heat of the moment she moved against his hand. Pleasure increased, intense heat, desire, need. She moaned, clutching his shoulders for fear she'd fall into a volcano. And then it came, hot and heavy. She cried out. He kissed her, smothering the sound. He stroked her gently until he pushed her over the edge and she was falling into such an intense orgasm it rocked her to the core.

He held her tightly until her body stopped trembling.

"Oh, my gosh," she said. "I can't… I didn't…" There were no words to describe it.

He groaned and suddenly he shot up and ungracefully tumbled her into the water, remembering to catch her at the last moment—barely. It jerked her back to reality.

"I…" He groaned and it wasn't from desire. Unceremoniously he hauled her up like a sack of flour. "Damn it. I didn't mean for that to happen." He glared at her as if it was all her fault.

"Neither did I. I didn't thrust my hands in your swimsuit."

Alex groaned. When she slipped, he grabbed for her again.

"I can take care of myself," Senetra snapped. "I didn't ask for this." Hauling herself up this time, she stomped from the tub, sloshing water over the side, and grabbed her robe. He followed right behind her.

When he reached for the door, she glared at him and he held up his hand, looking so damn sexy in his swim trunks she wanted to scream in frustration as desire shot through her again. That chest. Those powerful thighs. She grew weak in the knees just looking at him.

She just had to look elsewhere. She couldn't get down the hall to her room fast enough. Since they were the only guests, she'd left her room unlocked. Once inside, she slammed the door solidly behind her and twisted the lock.

"I'm falling into the same damn trap. I can't believe I did that." And enjoyed every second of it, her conscience nagged. She felt hot with embarrassment. He'd played her body like a fine-tuned instrument. Worse, he regretted it as much as she did. Did she regret it? Did she regret the first orgasm she'd ever had with a man? She'd always faked them with Timothy.

Senetra groaned. It was the drink. The two bottles of wine they'd consumed. What else could explain her ridiculous reaction?

Senetra moaned out loud. It felt like heaven in his arms. Goose bumps spread on her arms. She clenched her teeth against the ever-present desire. But guilt ate like acid in her stomach. She'd only taken what he'd offered and given him nothing in return. It was always one-sided with Timothy—all for him. He'd never put himself out to make sure she was sexually satisfied. She didn't want to be that kind of person.

But it wasn't as if Alex had *wanted* to make love with her. Afterward he'd dumped her in the tub as if she were a poisonous snake. Obviously he'd made as big a mistake as she had.

Alex closed his door quietly behind him and leaned against the cold, hard surface. He'd just kissed and intimately touched a married woman. That was so far from his moral code he couldn't quite wrap his mind around it. He had never dated, kissed or done anything else with married women.

But his body throbbed with unfulfilled desire. He balled his hands into fists.

It was the wine. That was his excuse and he was sticking to it. But he couldn't wrap his mind around it. He was going to burn in hell.

He heard her moving around next door. He had gotten

no release and his body was tense. Just thinking about her curves… *Don't even go there, buddy, or you'll be up the rest of the night,* he told himself.

Raking his hands over his head, he drew in a deep breath, headed to the shower and turned the water on cold.

And she'd let him. She'd let him touch her, take intimate liberties as if she were as single as he.

But was she married?

There were scars on her arm. She wasn't wearing any makeup and he saw a faint scar on the side of her face a few moments ago when they were standing at the sliding door. As if they'd healed long ago, but left a lasting mark on her. Had she run away from the great Timothy Blain?

His temper flared. The thought of a man Timothy's size beating on a woman like Senetra made him want to lay the guy out cold. You never could tell about those things. Abuse happened to the rich, as well as the poor.

This was too much. The first complete week he'd taken off in two years and it had pitched downhill from the beginning. He'd come up here for relaxation, not to get mixed up in some soap opera. He hoped to hell she was single. Alex swiped his hand over his face. He had a hard time dealing with the fact that he'd made love to a married woman.

Alex was curious. Internet services were available at the B and B. After he showered, he booted the computer up and searched for Timothy Blain.

There were several hits. He clicked on some of the

articles. The society section mentioned he attended a function with a Lidia Smith. Another mentioned an award the city had given him and one mentioned that he spoke at a fund-raising seminar.

So maybe she wasn't married. Alex kept searching until he hit on an article that mentioned his contentious divorce.

She was divorced. Now Alex had all the information he needed. He logged off and headed to bed.

The next morning, Senetra felt as if she hadn't gotten a wink of sleep when she went in to breakfast. She dreaded seeing Alex again. He was already there and seated, but he stood when she approached the table, even pulled out her chair for her. She smiled her thanks as she sank into the soft cushion and mumbled a hasty morning greeting.

"Good. Both of you are here," the owner said with a sunny smile. "Your friends are having breakfast in bed. What will you two have?"

Senetra stifled a groan. They would have to suffer through a tense breakfast. They gave their order and the owner disappeared.

Alex reached over and placed his hand on top of hers. He appeared to have gotten no more sleep than she.

"I'm feeling pretty awkward this morning," he said.

He didn't look awkward, Senetra thought. Anything but. He wore a green, cable-knit sweater. It did amazing things for his body. Or was it that she was still…

"Look, I'm sorry about last night," he said. "I was completely out of line."

The cook returned and filled their juice and water glasses. When she walked away, Senetra said, "Me, too. Why don't we just let it go as a lapse in judgment?"

He nodded and lifted his hand. Senetra felt like rubbing the sparks away, but she merely reached for her juice glass.

"I think Kat is going to keep Rick locked up in the room the rest of the morning. Why don't we go cross-country skiing? Do you know how to ski?"

Senetra nodded. "I'd like that."

Dorothelia Jackson washed her hands after gardening Tuesday morning. It was a balmy eighty degrees and she hurried into her house to start the coffee machine.

With a cup of coffee in hand and the newspapers tucked under her arm, she made her way to the bistro table on her patio and eased into a chair. The only thing missing was her daughter. When Senetra taught in L.A., she'd plan something for the two of them to do over the weekend. Usually it was a Sunday, since Saturdays she usually spent with her friends.

Sometimes Senetra stopped by for dinner on her way home from school.

There was a new exhibit in town, and they usually went together.

She booted up her computer and searched for the latest Milwaukee paper. She always read the obituary section first, hoping her SOB son-in-law had kicked the bucket. That was the only way her daughter would be free of him. Dorothelia sent up a quick prayer of apology for such evil thoughts, but when a man made it impossible for her daughter to come home, well, he deserved no better. With her online subscription, she scoured every issue, and every day there were many other names, but not the name she searched for—Timothy Blain.

Heck, Timothy was a young man. She'd be long gone before he died. It was a senseless waste of time, but something compelled her to keep searching.

When a familiar face popped into view, she thought she had the wrong section. She lifted her gaze to the heading. Yes, it was the obituary, not the local news. And Timothy's face was front and center. A whole page was dedicated to him, and Dorothelia read the entire article before she glanced up.

Timothy's death had been attributed to an accidental fall. *How the heck did he fall to his death?* she wondered. Was he on a trip at the Grand Canyon or something? He certainly didn't fall from a roof. He didn't so much as mow a lawn, much less climb up on the roof to clean out gutters.

Dorothelia had missed the Monday paper and searched for it. One by one she glanced through the front page and local news until she reached the correct date. An article was on the front page. He'd died Saturday night, Dorothelia read.

"Will wonders never cease? The devil got his due." His girlfriend-of-the-moment had accidentally pushed him down the stairs, it said. It probably happened while he was pulling her up the stairs by her hair to whip her butt, Dorothelia added, although the paper hadn't mentioned that. He'd broken his neck in the fall. Lucky guy.

Dorothelia sent up another prayer for her blasphemous thoughts. It wasn't glorying in the misfortune of others, she told herself. He'd taken her daughter away and she was feeling no love.

She stood so quickly she felt dizzy and plopped back into the seat. Her heart leaped with anticipation.

Senetra could come home. Senetra *was* coming home. Dorothelia was bubbling with so much joy she couldn't contain it. She leaped up, danced around the patio and caught a new neighbor staring at her. Dorothelia waved and ran inside to phone her friend.

"Rachel, the bastard's dead," she rushed out before the woman could offer a greeting.

"What bastard?" Rachel asked. She thought most men fit that category.

"Timothy Blain. Who else? He's dead."

"Thank God."

"My baby's coming home. But how will I get her the good news? I don't know where she is."

"She probably reads the paper online."

"I don't think so. The authorities told her not to make any connection that would link her with Milwaukee. He's found her before, you know. I don't think she'd take the risk."

"How would she find out, then?"

Dorothelia sighed. "I don't know."

"Give it a few days. See what happens."

"I have to believe she'd find out some way." She sucked in a breath and shouted for joy. "Oh, my gosh. She's finally coming home."

"Get dressed. I'm taking you out to celebrate."

* * *

Alex hadn't seen Senetra since their trip, and damn it, he couldn't forget her. For just a split second when she got out of the water and before she slipped on the robe, he saw more scars and wondered again what had caused them. There were two reasons people left their homes and assumed new identities. Either they were in the witness protection program or they were on the run. Alex wondered which was the case with Senetra. He was tempted to call his cousin to learn more about her situation.

Every day since their weekend he wondered if her husband had beaten her. Timothy Blain was well connected. If he was abusive, Senetra would have had no option but to leave and assume another identity.

Thoughts of Senetra/Regina invaded both his sleep and his waking hours. Her moans racked his nerves. Heck, that wasn't surprising when you were cooped up on Kodiak Island with a bunch of hardheads watching for polar bears and fishing. Two days of that was all he could take. Soon, he'd be back to work, dreaming of a woman's touch—Senetra's touch. Jessica was now relegated to a distant memory.

Lord, help him. He couldn't help being as intrigued by Mrs. Senetra Blain, aka Regina Novak, as he'd been the first time he'd seen her three years ago. He found himself packing up his gear and telling his group adios. He needed one more encounter with Senetra Blain before he returned to work. In his mind, he'd blown her way out of proportion. Reality couldn't be half as good as the dream.

* * *

On Wednesday, Danya Kirill's boat returned and on her way from school, Senetra drove toward the marina. For the first few hours the men would have been busy, but the catch should have been unloaded by now. Senetra rounded a bend and stomped down hard on her brakes. A huge black bear stood in her path. She debated turning around, but obviously the bear had an agenda of its own.

The bear disappeared into the bushes, heading back to the mountains. It must have already raided someone's trash can.

She heard a knock on her window and startled. Recognizing Alex, she lowered it.

"You okay?"

"Yes, thank you. I stopped to let the bear cross the road." She stifled a groan. He looked so good and sexy. Her senses tingled with awareness.

"You can report it when you get home. The place is fairly infested with bears this time of year."

"More than I want to see. But I guess we're invading their space." He had pretty brown eyes. She'd noticed them while they were skiing.

"That's one way of looking at it. Have dinner with me. I know a nice little seafood place."

Sit across from him over a meal? She didn't think so. She was off men, even if her insides clawed with need—wanting another hot orgasm the likes of which he had given her in the hot tub. Senetra looked away and her gaze settled on that hand. That hand that knew how to touch her. No way. It was thirty degrees outside, but she was hot as hell right now. She turned off the heater.

"I have errands to run," she finally said.

"After your errands. Tell me what time to pick you up."

She hesitated. She hadn't been out with a man in ages—except the weekend with him. And their love-making still unnerved her even though he'd apologized the next morning and they'd had a wonderful time skiing. He was great company, but still…

"Do I need to apologize for the hot tub again? I kind of lost it in there. The stars, the aurora borealis. Everything. We'll be around people. I won't lose my head again."

Senetra stifled a groan. He did have to mention that. She turned even hotter with desire and embarrassment. She couldn't count on not losing her head. She bit her bottom lip.

"You've already apologized enough," she managed to say.

"Strictly platonic," he said. "I'll even talk Rick into bringing Kat if it'll make you feel better. I won't even try to sneak a kiss."

She laughed. "Can I hold you to that?"

He held up a hand. "Scout's honor."

"You were a Scout, weren't you? You aren't fibbing?"

"Of course I was. It's just dinner."

Maybe it was time to get on the wagon again with someone who'd soon leave. It might be another ten months before he visited again.

"I thought you were going to Hawaii."

"Change of plans," he said with a smile. "I spent a couple of days at Kodiak, but after I got back Rick roped me into talking to the kids tomorrow."

Senetra hedged. "I really don't date. And you need to know up front there won't be a repeat of Saturday night."

"Consider me warned. No date. Just dinner." All innocence, he grinned. "I'm harmless."

They were all harmless in the beginning. He was anything but harmless in the hot tub.

"You're going to let me stand out here in the open when a bear could come along and have me for dinner?"

"We have to get out of the road." She'd completely forgotten where they were.

He tapped the roof. "Pick you up at six," he said, and loped back to his car without waiting for her response.

She hadn't said yes and she hadn't given him her address, but then she really didn't need to.

Senetra didn't go by the marina after all. Danya Kirill would be exhausted from the trip and probably not in the best of temper. Besides, the man was surely eager to get home to his family.

After much debate, she dressed for dinner in black slacks and a turquoise sweater. She tied a colorful scarf around her neck, and gazed out the window. It was pouring rain. She reached inside the closet for a slicker and placed it across the chair. Driving rain was a common occurrence in the costal area.

Alex arrived five minutes later.

"It's messy out there," he said. "I'll be happy to get takeout."

"Since when did a little rain keep anyone in?" she asked as she donned her long blue slicker and led the way out of the apartment. She left the lights on in the living room and locked the dead bolt before they left.

Outside, his car was parked several spaces down from the front door. He held an umbrella over their heads, but the rain was driving sideways and splattered them anyway as they ran to the vehicle. It took them less than a minute to reach the restaurant.

Her mind flashed back to another time with Timothy and paranoia gripped her.

"Are you okay?" Alex asked, his brow furrowed in concern. "Would you prefer to go someplace else?"

Senetra inhaled slowly, trying to think calmly as if she wasn't about to run screaming down the street like a crazy woman.

"The food is exquisite here, but this wasn't a good idea," she managed to mutter.

"What's wrong? Plenty of empty seats." Alex gently moved her to the side so others could pass, but he didn't let her go. He stroked her arm softly as if calming a frightened kitten.

"I shouldn't be here."

"I sensed something was wrong the other night. Wanna talk about it?" he asked soothingly. "I'm a good listener."

"It's just… You're a stranger. I…"

"We aren't strangers—exactly."

Her nerves shattered. "What do you mean?"

"Kat wouldn't have invited me on the trip if I posed a threat."

If Senetra continued along this vein, he was going to get suspicious. What was she thinking? He was already suspicious. The sudden panic attack confused and frightened her. She couldn't control the nervousness. She'd never had a panic attack before.

"Ms. Novak," Mark said, approaching them.

Senetra smiled at him as if he were a lifeline pulling her to safety. "Hello," she responded too eagerly.

"Hello, Mr. Wilson."

Alex mumbled a greeting around a frown, and Senetra smiled to cover his rudeness.

Mark shoved his hands deep in his pockets. "My dad's back."

"I saw *The Tempest* docked at the Spit." The tightness in her chest began to ease. "I'll talk to him soon."

"He moved out," he said in mild disbelief. "My mom signed the papers. They had a huge fight about it. I don't think I can go." His thin shoulders slumped. "I don't want to destroy my parents' marriage. Mom and Dad need each other."

"Oh, Mark. I'm so sorry."

"Dad hasn't gotten over Viktor's death. He needs me."

"It's too soon." Senetra touched his arm lightly.

"I know. I loved my brother. It's hard on me, too—on

everyone." He shrugged and gazed off to the sea. "I...I just don't know what to do."

His voice was so forlorn Senetra wanted to hug him and tell him all would be fine, but life didn't work that way.

"Your dad needs time to work through his grief," she said. "Just send the papers. By September he could have a change of heart."

"I don't know," he muttered. "Anyway, have a nice dinner," he muttered, and ambled away.

"I've met Mark's parents," Alex said. "They've really had a bad blow."

Senetra nodded.

"You okay?" Alex's gaze flickered over her, then focused on Mark's retreat.

"I'm fine," she said, the words rushing out on a breath. The conversation with Mark had chased the panic away. Sighing, she went inside and waited to be seated.

She understood Danya Kirill's problem. It was hard letting fear go. She was allowing her own fear to destroy her evening. But if she didn't take that first step, she'd be a hostage forever. She'd take things one step at a time.

This wasn't a date, but she could at least try to enjoy her meal.

Several days had passed and Dorothelia still hadn't heard from Senetra. She was going to have to find her. She was desperate to hear her daughter's voice. In the

den she pulled out the paperwork on Senetra's donor
father.

All week she'd wondered if Senctra had enjoyed her
birthday. Had she spent it alone or had friends helped
her celebrate? Dorothelia had purchased a gift, just as
she'd bought a Christmas gift, hoping that one day soon,
she'd have the opportunity to give them to her. Above
all she hoped her daughter was happy and thriving.

She dialed the number and listened.

"Hello, is this the Avery residence?"

"Yes, it is," a pleasant female voice responded.

"May I speak to Mr. Avery, please?"

"One moment, please."

Dorothelia twisted the cord while she waited. It
seemed at least five minutes had passed before she was
greeted by a soothing male voice.

"Mr. Avery," she said. "My name is Dorothelia Jackson. I apologize for troubling you. I don't know if you
remember me, but I told my daughter about you last
summer and wondered if she contacted you." Dorothelia
knew she wasn't making sense, but she was so nervous.

"I'm sorry, I don't know what you're talking
about."

How could he have forgotten their meeting? It was
the turning point in her life, but not in his, she reminded
herself. Dorothelia took a calming breath. The man
probably thought she was a babbling idiot instead of a
woman who had managed a business for over thirty
years. "My daughter was forced into hiding. I told her

you were her donor father and that you gave her permission to contact you."

"You're talking about my son, Mackenzie."

"Oh."

"Mackenzie's dead."

"I'm so sorry."

"Tell me about your situation. Why did your daughter go into hiding?"

Dorothelia felt horrible. This poor man was grieving and she was intruding. "I shouldn't be troubling you…."

"Please, Ms. Jackson. I'd like to help you."

"Her husband was abusive. She filed for divorce and signed the papers just before she left. While she was in town, he found her…." She gathered a breath. "He'd tracked her down once before, but this time he tried to kill her. He didn't know about your son. I told her about him and I thought maybe he'd help her."

"I would have, had she come to me. Where is she now?"

She sighed. "I don't know. Her ex-husband died recently and she's free to come home, but I don't think she knows. I don't know how to find her."

"Mrs. Jackson, please come to Virginia and I'll help you find your daughter. And your husband is welcome, too."

"My husband died many years ago, but I'm a stranger—"

"You're my granddaughter's mother," he stated firmly. "I'll have a car pick you up from the airport.

When can you come?" he asked, not giving her a chance to think this through.

"I'll try to catch the first flight out tomorrow."

"Call me back with the flight information. We'll find your daughter, Mrs. Jackson," he said with confidence, and hung up.

Dorothelia placed the phone on the hook. She was out of her mind going to a strange place to meet a strange man. She should call him back and tell him she'd changed her mind, but she didn't have a clue on how to find Senetra.

Dorothelia's hand hovered above the phone. He really didn't need her there. They could communicate by phone or the Internet, but for some reason he wanted her there. And he accepted Senetra as his granddaughter without wavering or proof. What kind of man did that?

Dorothelia knew. Mackenzie had truly been his father's son. Mackenzie had been so kind. She'd met him once. He was such a young man, no more than twenty-two, that she felt guilty for using his sperm to conceive and told him so. Usually the donor didn't meet the host. Their situation was unusual. But he'd calmed her and she'd told him how desperately she and her husband wanted a child. In return he'd divulged information about his family's Thoroughbred farm and that he was studying to become a veterinarian. When he talked about his career choice she knew he loved animals. Senetra had loved animals, too, although she didn't have her donor father's desire to become a vet. She inherited his gentleness, though. Such a gentle and caring man must have come from a strong and good family.

Dorothelia was going to Virginia.

George Avery hung up the phone with a smile on his face. Another granddaughter. God, how he was blessed.

"Leila," he shouted.

His housekeeper, Leila Nelson, ran in from the kitchen with a dish towel in her hand. "What is it, George?"

"Prepare the best guest room. Company's coming tomorrow."

"For how long?"

George shrugged. "I don't know."

"You're getting ready for the Kentucky Derby," Leila said, disgruntled. "How are you going to entertain for any length of time?"

"Whatever it takes." He couldn't contain a smile. "Congratulate me. I have another granddaughter."

"How many of them are there?" she asked suspiciously.

"I don't know, and the center won't tell me."

"At the rate you're going, you could end up with twenty or thirty."

"And I'll welcome every one of them."

How his life had changed since he discovered he had grandchildren. His son had died only months before the first one, Noelle, appeared in his life. His wife had been dead for years. He'd hit bottom. He had nothing to live for. If it wasn't for Colin, his best friend's grandson, he would have wilted.

George smiled. And now he had not two, but *three* granddaughters.

"Leila, make sure the guest room is stocked with everything she might want. I want her to get the best treatment."

"Don't you think you should call your lawyer?"

"I'm sure you will." George's lawyer had insisted on the paperwork confirming the two grandchildren who'd contacted them, Noelle and Jasmine.

Leila sent him a saccharine smile. "I'll get on it right away." As much as Leila tried to impersonate the hard-nosed voice of reason, she was as taken with the girls as he was. From the beginning, they'd wrapped her around their pinkies. But his lawyer had scolded him for making decisions without first running them by him.

George didn't need a piece of paper to tell him these young ladies were his. He saw his wife, Margaret, and his son, Mackenzie, in each one. It was funny the way neither girl had met his wife, but Noelle had her smile, and Jasmine had her eyes and serious demeanor. They weren't actually girls. They were women. Wonderful women, if he said so himself.

He suddenly remembered this young woman had disappeared because of someone who abused her. *Just give me five minutes with that boy,* George thought, burning hot with anger. Somebody should have taught the SOB how to treat women long ago. Now it was too late for him to learn, but that wasn't his problem. He had a granddaughter and he was going to find her.

Once he got the details from Mrs. Jackson, he'd hire the private investigator he'd used in the past to find her. The firm was very good.

Dorothelia. What a lovely name to match an equally lovely voice. She must be a young woman, probably not much older than his son. But there was something about her voice that stirred desire in him he thought was long buried. *George, my boy, you're too old to feel these things for a woman you haven't even met.* He never was the kind to chase young skirts and he certainly wasn't going to start now.

George sighed. There was something mesmerizing, something pleasing about Dorothelia's voice.

Chapter 5

It was two weeks after Senetra's birthday weekend and she still looked back on it with happiness. The middle of March was still pretty cold, although it had warmed up a little. Senetra considered looking for a husky puppy again, but gnawed on the same old dilemma. The poor dog would be cooped up in the apartment all day while she was at school. It wasn't as if doggie day care was as available here as it was in larger cities in the lower forty-eight.

She could walk the dog before school and again after she returned home, but it wasn't fair. Eventually she would buy a house with a doggie door and it could frolic in the fenced-in backyard. Perhaps she'd buy two dogs.

They could keep each other company during the day, but until then… She wanted some companionship.

Senetra passed teens holding hands in the school hallway and sighed with resignation. Young love. She tried not to think of Alex, but being with him had emphasized her aloneness. Close friends were a joy, but it wasn't the same.

At least she'd taken a step forward. Dinner had been pleasant and so had skiing. They'd even attended a barn dance Saturday night. And true to his word, they hadn't made love or really kissed. Before he'd left he'd kissed her on the cheek. Very chaste. Very friendly. He hadn't asked for her phone number and he hadn't called. But she'd missed him. And her body still craved his touch.

Senetra sighed in frustration.

"Ms. Novak, I need a letter of recommendation. Will you give me one?" one of her students asked.

"Of course. Give me the information on where to send it and leave it in my box."

"We're supposed to give you a two-week notice, but I'm kinda late."

There was a running drama with seniors, getting them to stay on target with applications and recommendation letters. "When do you need it?"

The girl scrunched up her face. "In a week."

"I'll do it *this* time. But remember the rules," she warned, and softened it with a smile. What was she teaching the girl?

"Oh, thank you." The student ran down the hallway toward the office.

Senetra shook her head and almost barreled into Kathryn in the hallway. Two books slipped from Kathryn's arms. Senetra bent to pick them up.

"You're in a hurry," Senetra said, handing over the books.

"I can't wait to get home. Look, I'm glad I caught you. Rick and I are going to the Pit tonight. Want to join us?"

"I have karate after school. Then I'm taking a long, hot bath and reading a book in front of a fire."

"You can still do all that," Kathryn said. "Don't say no. It's karaoke night. Rick's going to sing and probably drag me up there with him. I don't want to be the only one making a fool out of myself." Once a month on Friday nights, the Pit had karaoke and it was their most popular night.

Senetra laughed. "I can't carry a tune."

"Say you'll come?"

"No. I'm going to read."

"For someone who loves to read romances, you certainly stay farther from relationships than anyone I know. Every single man in town is trying to get a date with you, and you turn them all down. It's a wonder you had dinner with Alex, but he's so nice."

"I'm not looking for a relationship, Kathryn. You know that. I'm trying to build my career."

"One doesn't have to be exclusive of the other, you know. People can walk and talk at the same time."

Senetra sighed in frustration. Kathryn was always trying to set her up with a blind date. "I enjoy my job. It takes a lot of my time."

"Only because you volunteer for everything. Some of the projects could be doled out to other teachers, you know. Now, I'll pick you up at nine. We'll have a ball."

"Kat—"

"Hang loose for a change."

"I need to clean my apartment. It's been two weeks since I gave it a good cleaning."

"What an exciting thing to do," Kathryn said sarcastically. "One more day isn't going to kill you. They're your germs." She backpedaled toward her classroom. "See you at nine."

Senetra blew out a long breath. It was hard telling Kathryn no. She never gave up.

Senetra had survived her first date since Timothy without making a complete fool of herself. Barely. This was a gathering of locals. So much for a relaxing evening in front of a fire.

She was still a little jittery about being around a lot of people, but she knew she needed to step out of her safe little haven. If she continued in the same vein, she'd soon become a hermit, only leaving home to work, and for karate.

At one time, she had wondered how people like Howard Hughes who led a fairly normal life ended up as hermits. For the last few months she found that quite easy.

Senetra left the building and headed to her Jeep. She felt safe within her four walls.

Both Charles and Senetra survived karate class without a mishap. And by the time Kathryn stopped by her apartment, Senetra had at least cleaned the living room and kitchen and had a short soak in the tub. She'd sleep late tomorrow and finish cleaning. Then she'd have the rest of the day to herself. She was thinking about going to the dock to buy some clams to make clam chowder since she wasn't going to grade papers until Sunday after church.

She glanced at the fireplace wistfully. The logs were staked up, ready to be lit. Maybe she'd start a fire when she returned and relax over a cup of tea.

She couldn't help wondering if Alex had taken a quick trip to Wisconsin. His father seemed anxious to see him.

"I can't believe you actually cleaned," Kathryn said, inching her way in the door. "The orange scent hit me in the hallway."

"Less to do tomorrow," Senetra said as she grabbed her coat, hat and gloves and headed out.

Alex was the first face she saw when they entered the bar, minutes later. Her heart gladdened, but she contained her joy.

"What's he doing here?" Senetra asked. He had just left a couple of weeks ago. She thought they worked longer before taking leave.

"He's here for the weekend."

"You should have told me you were trying to set me up again."

"Don't be angry. Didn't you enjoy his company before?"

"That's beside the point," Senetra said as Rick tapped the bar.

"Another bar fight, Grant?" Rick said, frowning.

Grant shook his head and laughed. "My face just keeps getting in the way. How you'all doing?" he asked as he deftly mixed drinks.

"You've got to learn to duck in time," Kathryn said as they headed to Alex's table.

The music was already loud and a couple of dancers were on the floor. In the back room a group was playing pool.

Her gaze met Danya Kirill's as he nursed a drink at the end of the bar. His gaze strayed from Senetra to his wife.

A lump formed in Senetra's stomach. She hadn't intended to cause a rift between husband and wife. She should have minded her own business.

Iris sat laughing with a few friends, but she was watching Danya, too. It was apparent they loved each other deeply, but each was too stubborn to breach the rift.

Alex stood as they neared his table, dragging Senetra's gaze from the troubled couple. He looked as sexy as ever. His sleeves were pushed up nearly to his elbows, exposing his forearms.

Alex regarded Senetra and he knew why he was back so soon, why he'd jumped at any excuse. Obviously she hadn't expected to see him. He smiled.

"Welcome back," Kathryn said, opening her arms for a hug. "Now Regina has a dance partner. I won't feel guilty when I'm on the floor."

Senetra wanted to hit her. She could find a dance partner if she wanted one.

Alex and Rick shook hands before Alex held out a chair for Senetra, muttered a soft hello and briefly kissed her on the lips. The air around her felt electrified. He smelled of masculine soap and pure him.

"Heck, there're always dance partners for women," Rick moaned. "It's the men who have the problem."

The guys easily outnumbered the women three to one.

They soon had drinks in front of them. While everyone else had ordered alcoholic beverages, Senetra drank a club soda.

"How was your trip?" she asked.

"It was good." Alex leaned back in his seat and caught a light whiff of Senetra's perfume. It was driving him slowly insane.

"So you and Regina going to sing tonight?" Rick asked. "They're starting up with the karaoke."

"We're going to leave that to you." The first couple sang a country-and-Western ballad about lost love. The next song had a livelier beat.

"You just want to watch me get booed off the floor."

"Come on." Kathryn pulled Rick onto the floor, but Senetra was watching Danya Kirill. Was she planning on approaching him tonight? The man was drinking. It wasn't the best time.

"I thought they kept you oil guys locked up for weeks at a time."

Alex shifted his chair closer so they could hear each other over the loud music. "For the first year and a half

I worked for months with just an occasional day off, but now I'm taking more leave."

"It's good you have that option," she said.

"Actually, I'm here for the king salmon competition tomorrow. Rick and I are going out with four other guys."

"Have you done this before?"

"Not this particular one, but I've gone deep-sea fishing with them."

"Well, I'll be at the dock cheering."

His gaze roamed her pretty face. She'd applied a touch of makeup. His eyes traveled down her smooth neck to the V in her blouse covered with an open sweater. Heat burned her cheeks and he smiled knowingly. "I'll be looking for you in the crowd."

She shifted uneasily in her seat and sipped on her drink.

"It's Rick and Kathryn's turn to sing," she said, attempting to divert his attention.

Alex leaned back, placing his arm around the back of Senetra's chair, and they settled back to listen. Rick and Kathryn sang "That Loving Feeling" with every bit of the drama that Tom Cruise had put into it. But they weren't booed off. When they returned to the table, Kathryn pulled each of them up.

"Your turn," she said.

At the mike, they sang an old seventies song. It was a soulful melody and by the time they finished, every eye was on them. The laughter had been replaced by wistful expressions. Iris quickly dabbed tears from her eyes. This time Alex peered at Danya. Through the thick beard, he could barely see the man's thin lips tighten with anger and pain.

Some of the schoolkids were in the back room playing the game machines.

"I didn't know you could sing like that, Ms. Novak," Mark said, grabbing their attention as they headed to their seats.

Senetra paused. "I used to sing in the church choir. Of course, I wasn't the lead singer. There were so many who were better."

That figured, Alex thought before she tightened up as if she'd let something slip that shouldn't have. But what was so secretive about singing in church? This woman intrigued him. She was a mystery he wanted to solve. And it wasn't because there weren't many women where he worked, he thought with a touch of humor. There were more women in Anchorage, and he had friends there, even female friends. But none of them had intrigued him as much as this woman.

It was near midnight when they decided they should have nourishment to go with the drinks. "Caribou omelet for dinner?" Senetra asked when Alex ordered it.

"It's really good here, any time of the day."

"I'm ordering a lobster sandwich. I can't picture myself eating a cute caribou."

"It's delicious," Alex murmured around a grin. "You should try it."

"Carnivore."

"Don't tell me you're tuning into a vegan. I can just picture lobster frolicking freely through the water."

"Maybe I should go vegetarian."

He raised his eyebrows, a grin playing around his lips. "And miss all this great food?"

"You've got a point," she said.

While they waited for their dinner, Alex pulled her out on the dance floor when a slow song began playing. Senetra was beginning to feel relaxed against the warmth of Alex's chest when Danya's slurred voice reached him.

"It's all your fault," Danya bellowed, his tone almost drowning out the music.

Okay, this was where she was supposed to gear herself up to use her nonexistent karate. Danya's size made at least five of her. She could karate herself from here to Wisconsin and it wouldn't be enough to take Danya down, not with her limited knowledge.

Maybe she should position herself anyway, but she was so nervous, all her training flew right out her head. She couldn't even think clearly. *Okay, okay. Take a deep breath.* She couldn't close her eyes to concentrate. Danya could flatten her on the floor while she pulled herself together. Lord, have mercy. All this training, and for what? She was ill equipped to deal with her first confrontation.

"Danya. Why don't we make an appointment for Monday after school and we can discuss this?" she said. She realized she had to talk around Alex because he'd positioned himself between her and Danya. She moved to his side. She wouldn't hide behind Alex.

"Appointment. Appointment." Danya threw up his hands. "That's all you do is set up appointments. Or waylaying me at my ship. Well, appointments can't fix crap. We're going to settle this right here. Right now," he growled, pointing his finger at the floor for emphasis.

The one thing Senetra knew was you couldn't argue with a drunk.

"Let's talk about it tomorrow, then," Senetra said.

"I want to talk now," Danya demanded.

Alex felt the moment Senetra stiffened and tried to put her behind him, but although she was frightened, she wouldn't go.

"You've had too much to drink," Alex said. "Why don't you go home?"

"Because I'm talking to her now," he said, his booming voice drowning out the music, and others began to intercede and urge him to a seat. But he shook them off as if they were no more than pesky mosquitoes. Even Grant, with his busted shoulder, had inserted himself between them.

"Danya Kirill." A slip of a woman whipped up to him, pushing him in the chest. "You leave her alone. It's your own stubborn fault. Go home." Iris put herself between everyone and the ox, but he ceremoniously picked her clean off the floor and set her gently to the side, as if she weighed no more than a porcelain doll.

"I've got a few things to say to her, Missy. You stay out of it."

"If you pick me up again, I'm going to clobber you," Iris said, whacking him in the chest and boldly putting herself between them again. "Mark, take your dad home."

In his wife's presence, Danya seemed more a teddy bear than a bear, but Senetra was shaking slightly in Alex's arms and trying to hide her fear. Alex tightened one arm around her and for the first time, took his gaze off Danya and got a clear look at her face. He tried to reassure her with his gaze, but it didn't work.

"Come on, Dad. You drank too much," Mark said, urging him toward the door.

"I just…" The man scratched his head. "I wanna talk to her."

"You can't talk to her," Mark said, easing him toward the door, but Danya kept trying to walk back. Mark kept him moving toward the door.

"I'm sorry, Senetra," Iris said. "He's as harmless as a teddy bear, but when he drinks he has to have his say. This thing is between us, not you. I should have put my foot down a long time ago."

Alex had moved her beside him now, and though Senetra was still shaking, she nodded.

"Oh, honey. You're pale as can be. He wouldn't hurt a flea. I'm the spitfire in the family."

Senetra tried to smile, but it was the saddest reflection of a smile Alex had ever seen.

"She'll be okay," Alex said. "I'm going to take her outside for fresh air."

"You do that. I'm going to give that man a good talking-to for approaching you like that."

"I'm fine," Senetra finally muttered, pinching her lips to keep them from trembling. "Really."

Everyone else had resumed dancing, but Alex literally put Senetra into her coat and led her outside. As soon as she got there, she threw up in the bushes. This was more serious than he thought.

"He wasn't going to harm you. And even if he tried, I wasn't going to let him get near you. They all know him," Alex tried to soothe as he guided her inside Rick's truck and warmed up the motor. A minute later, Rick came outside with their food packed in take-out boxes.

"Is she okay?" Rick asked Alex.

"She will be. I'm going to take her home. Ride with me so you can bring the truck back."

Rick climbed into the backseat and they were off.

Alex kept watching Senetra. She didn't say anything, merely hovered by the door. Now he believed more than ever that she'd been the product of spousal abuse and had divorced Timothy. She was clearly hiding out.

Just get me home, Senetra thought. *And I'll be okay.* The building was secure. She had extra locks on the door. Her gun was in the drawer by her bed. Once she got home, she'd be fine.

Her shoulders sagged in defeat. Who was she kidding? If Danya Kirill wanted in, all he had to do was stand by the front door until someone he knew came and they'd just let him in. Everyone knew each other here.

What on earth was she thinking to move here? She'd worked herself into a false sense of security. She wasn't safe anywhere. Any disgruntled or drunk person could attack her, not just Timothy. A woman just wasn't safe.

She jumped when Alex opened her door to help her out.

She was so out of it she didn't realize she was home. She was soon inside her apartment, but she still shivered with cold.

"Why don't I light a fire?" Alex said.

"You can go. I'll be fine." She was embarrassed for her cowardice.

"I can't leave you like this," he said gently, kneeling in front of the fireplace and lighting the wood already set there. In minutes flames were licking the logs—and she was still standing in the middle of the floor, her coat clutched tightly around her.

Alex stood, wondering how he should proceed. He saw a thick throw across the sofa. Shrugging out of his coat, he placed it across a chair and slowly walked toward her, talking gently. "I'm going to take your coat and hang it up for you. Maybe you can snuggle up in the throw. Can I get you some hot chocolate or something?" he asked.

Senetra shook her head, but let him take her coat.

"I'm used to being alone. I can take care of myself," she insisted.

"I know you can. I'm not taking care of you. I just want to spend some time with you. It's the reason I'm here."

"If you think—"

"No pressure," Alex insisted, or else she'd send him packing and he really didn't want to leave her like this. "Just friendship."

While she debated her next move, he led her to the sofa and they both snuggled under the blanket. He eased his arm around her shoulder, waiting for her to reject him, but she didn't. The fire began to heat the room and Alex was soon too hot, forcing him to shed his sweater, but Senetra was still shivering slightly, although not as much as before.

For it to affect her this long, she must have lived a nightmare. And he'd thought she had everything in Milwaukee.

Her reaction also explained the fine lines of scars on her body. If he gave himself a chance, his anger would blossom out of control, so he gathered a breath and held it inside. Who didn't know abuse occurred and the laws still weren't enough to protect women? How many times did he read about a woman being killed the night before she was to go to court, even when she'd taken out a restraining order against her partner? And Senetra was hiding out, away from her family, the ones she loved, to protect herself from Timothy. It was enough to make a person believe in vigilante justice. But then you'd have chaos.

Alex pulled Senetra closer and rubbed her arms. How could Timothy have done that to such a lovely woman? How could anyone do this and live with himself?

Chapter 6

Senetra thought she was getting better, that she'd put the past behind her. It only took one incident to throw her back into her nightmarish past.

She was still on the sofa reclining beside Alex. She'd pulled off her shoes hours ago. She blew out a long breath.

She was angry and disappointed with herself for coming unglued. Sure, there was danger in the world, but everyone wasn't going to beat her to a pulp as Timothy had. And his cronies weren't hiding behind every bush, waiting to take her to him.

She wouldn't let Timothy ruin her life. How many times had she told herself that? Okay, enough of that. She'd learned not to beat herself up the way Timothy had every time she made a mistake as if she was supposed to be perfect. She'd keep practicing her karate until she got it right. And when she really needed it, perhaps it would come forth.

Senetra stuck her chin in the air. She wasn't helpless. One error didn't negate everything she'd learned or become. She'd started a new life. She was well liked by the people in the community. She was okay.

She gazed at Alex. He was sleeping soundly, his arm thrown over her waist. Sometime during the night they'd eaten some of the food.

Surprisingly, he hadn't asked any questions, but he must be wondering what caused her reaction. Truthfully, she was glad he'd come home with her. She'd let him stay because she was afraid Danya was coming after her.

She looked around the room. It smelled of wood smoke and orange blossoms. Good thing she'd cleaned the living room yesterday, she thought. She eased from under the covers and made her way to the bathroom. After brushing her teeth and washing her face, she gave the bathroom a thorough cleaning and put out a toothbrush, washcloth and towel for Alex.

When she returned, Alex was still sleeping. Senetra made her way to the kitchen and started breakfast. While the sausage and bacon were sizzling, Alex came into the kitchen, looking tall and handsome. His hair was mussed and his clothing wrinkled, none of which detracted from his attractiveness.

She felt foolish. Would he ask questions now? He

had to have questions about her actions, but she hoped he was discreet enough to let it ride.

Senetra smiled. "I put some things out for you in the bathroom," she said. "But my soap is kind of feminine."

He grinned. "I can live with that."

They laughed, and Senetra relaxed a little more. He wasn't going to ask questions she wasn't ready to answer, although she knew he must be curious.

"Thanks for staying. By the time you're through, breakfast should be ready. Unfortunately, I don't have the fixings for a caribou omelet, but if you would prefer the leftovers I'll heat them up."

"Whatever you're cooking will be fine."

Her eyes were still on him as he turned and walked down the short hallway.

Surprisingly, the bathroom was pretty roomy for an apartment, with his-and-her sinks. After brushing his teeth, Alex took a quick shower. He wondered how long Senetra had been up and if she'd let him kiss her again.

In the kitchen the food smelled delicious and Alex realized he was quite hungry.

As Senetra placed a platter on the table, he gathered her in his arms and nuzzled her neck.

"Are you going to let me kiss you?" he asked.

"I…"

He kissed her behind the ear. "Hmm?"

She moaned.

"Like that?" he asked, smoothing kisses along her

cheek until he turned her in his arms and kissed her fully on the mouth.

"I like," she breathed, and he deepened the kiss, tasting the sweetness of her.

He inched his hand beneath her sweater, feeling the softness of her back. "Am I going too fast for you?"

"Noooo. But you're confusing me."

He kissed her collarbone, her neck and back to her lips, his hands and fingers exploring her softness.

"You've confused me from the moment I met you," he said.

Senetra felt as if she were going to explode with the delightfulness of his touch. She slipped her hands beneath his shirt and stroked the tense muscles, the texture of his skin—and inhaled sharply.

"You smell like me."

"As long as you're pleased," he said before he pushed her blouse aside to caress the peak of her breast. "I'm up for being kidded by the guys."

Senetra moaned out loud.

"Woman, if we don't stop now, it's going to be damn hard later."

"Oh." She looked confused, the arousal from their foreplay evident on her face and the memories of two weeks ago still singing through her veins.

Alex wanted to go with the mood. But he wasn't sure she was ready for that again. There were a lot of unresolved issues around Senetra. And he wanted to make sure she was in bed with him and not a memory.

He couldn't deny himself one last kiss.

"Your breakfast is getting cold," he said, closing her

blouse and stepping back from her. He tucked his hands in his pockets to keep from reaching for her again.

Her skin was pleasantly flushed and Alex wanted to drag her back into his arms and take things to another level, but he reminded himself once again she wasn't anywhere near ready for that.

"Breakfast looks good, by the way."

"Okay." She stepped back and tugged on her blouse to straighten it.

"Why don't I nuke the food? You have a seat." Alex needed to do something to calm the desire still raging through his body.

"I'll help."

"No." Alex kissed her on the forehead. "I need to do this, baby. Just…sit."

Senetra eased into the chair and watched Alex as he deftly warmed the food and set platters on the table. She poured the coffee, wondering what the heck she was getting into. She should send him away, but knew she couldn't. They'd gone too far for that. Besides, she really did like him.

He sat in the chair across from her and filled his plate to brimming. Senetra was too unsettled to eat, but dished up a little for hers.

Alex ate a quarter of the food on his plate before he set his fork aside while Senetra had merely managed to sip her coffee.

"It's time we got a few things straight," he said.

"Like what?"

"I don't expect you to tell me the history of your life until you feel comfortable enough to trust me, but the tournament isn't the only reason I'm here. It's not even the main reason," he said.

Senetra sighed. She'd gathered that much.

"I came because there's something powerful between us that I want to explore."

"I—"

"I know you said you aren't ready for a serious relationship and I'm not pushing you, but it's not always a matter of when we're ready, but when the right person comes into your life. And for now, that's what I feel for you."

"I won't lie to you and deny my feelings. I wouldn't have let you touch me the way you did two weeks ago if I wasn't attracted to you, but…I don't know."

He took her hand in his and stroked the back.

"You know, I thought after I broke up with my girlfriend a couple years ago that I'd never find anyone that was as good as what I had. And now I've found something I think could be better. I think I was more in love with the idea of family with her," he said. "Life is funny, you know. When you least suspect it, it turns on you."

"I can't promise you anything."

"I'm not asking for promises. Let's just take this time and explore. Maybe tour the area together. Fish. Ski. Whatever you like," he said. "Or go pick out the puppy you were set on buying."

They both laughed.

"I've changed my mind about the husky—for now anyway. It's not fair to keep a dog like that cooped up in here."

"I've worked really hard the last couple of years," Alex said. "Now I want to take a little time on the weekends for me."

"I don't want to disappoint you in the end. I don't want to give you false hope."

"We can be friends if nothing else."

Senetra nodded and picked up her fork. "Okay."

They ate and were relaxing over a second cup of coffee.

"So, it's over with your friend in Wisconsin? Completely over?" Senetra asked. "You aren't on the rebound, are you?"

Alex paused before he said, "No."

Senetra gave him an uneasy glance. "You don't sound sure."

"I was on the verge of asking her to marry me."

Senetra didn't usually ask questions because she didn't want to answer questions about her past. But she was curious, especially if they were going to move forward.

She decided to make sure he didn't expect more than she could offer. "I can't promise you anything, Alex."

"Meaning?"

"Any kind of future. I just deal with day to day."

"So I can at least visit you when I get leave?"

"For now. And since I can't answer questions, I have no right to ask you any."

He leaned back in his chair, looking much too appealing. "As long as you're single, I have no problems at all."

She smiled. "I'm single."

"We don't have a problem, then," he said, leaning forward for his coffee cup. "Feel free to ask me anything you want. I have nothing to hide."

Senetra bit her lip. "There's no one else in my life. I don't want to start a relationship with you when someone back home might be waiting."

"No worries there. She's married. And she and her husband are expecting their first child."

Unrequited love could be a tricky thing. "Are you still in love with her?"

"No. It took a while, but it's over."

He was hurt. He'd been in love with this woman. Maybe he still was.

"What was her name?"

"Jessica. We went to high school together."

Even worse. It was a relationship of long duration.

They were both startled when the knocker at the door pinged.

Thinking it was Kathryn, Senetra got up to answer it. But as soon as the door opened, Danya's huge form filled up the doorway and she gasped.

"Hi." Iris's perky voice was a welcome gift. Mark was standing on the other side, nearly out of view, but Senetra couldn't seem to relax until she felt Alex beside her.

"Come in, please," Alex said, and put his arm around Senetra to move her aside.

"We won't stay," Iris said, "but Danya has something to say."

The huge man lumbered inside, clearly disgruntled. "She knew I wouldn't hurt her, Iris," he said to his wife.

"I don't know why you're making such a big deal out of it. Not the first time I've been drunk." He leveled a narrow gaze at her. "Wish I could instill a little fear in you."

"Will never happen, big guy, but you could give it your best shot. And you owe Ms. Novak an apology," she said, pointing to Senetra. "You scared her to death last night," Iris insisted.

Danya grunted again.

Alex could feel Senetra stiffen up. He tightened his arm around her, hoping to help her relax.

"I apologize, Ms. Novak. Didn't mean to frighten you." Then he looked at his wife. "Will that do?"

"Barely," the spitfire mumbled.

Senetra nodded, but Alex knew all she wanted was for Danya Kirill to leave her apartment.

"What happened between us had nothing to do with you, and Danya had no business blaming you. Right, Danya?" Iris said, elbowing him in the side.

Danya executed a curt nod, then glared at his wife.

"We won't hold you. Danya's taking me to breakfast. Then he's going to participate in the King Salmon Tournament. He and his brother are taking Mark and a couple of Mark's friends with them."

"Thanks for stopping by," Senetra said.

"You okay?" Alex asked after he closed the door behind them.

The only thing on Senetra's mind was she wasn't safe anywhere. They shouldn't have been able to get into a secure apartment so easily. She'd checked that out before she signed the lease. She now had proof she wouldn't even have any warning if Timothy came after her. He'd be at the apartment, breaking down her door before she could get to safety. But she couldn't go anywhere else.

"Regina?" Alex asked, rubbing her arm. "Are you okay, honey?"

Senetra hoped the smile she offered wasn't lopsided. "I'm fine."

"I wish I could spend the day with you, but remember I'm in the tournament, too."

"I remember. How many are on your boat?"

"There are six of us."

"It's Kat's favorite event. She's been talking about it for weeks. So we'll be at the Spit at four to cheer for you."

"We're going to have a lot to celebrate since we plan to catch the biggest king salmon."

"Right. I'll cheer you even when you bring in the tiniest one."

He got his coat from the closet. "You're gonna eat those words, woman. Save a dance for me. We're going to celebrate tonight." He smacked a kiss on her lips and was gone.

Senetra touched her lips where he'd planted the innocent kiss, wondering how long those chaste kisses were going to be sufficient when her body couldn't forget that one unforgettable night.

It was time, Senetra thought. She had to be willing to trust new relationships. Not all men were like Timothy. Now that she thought back on it, Danya had never done anything to make her think he would harm her. How many times had she heard Iris say how gentle he was and that he'd never hurt anyone? How many times had she heard Iris say she had to be the strong disciplinarian? That Danya was always too soft with the boys. When panic set in, it was impossible to think logically.

Poor guy. Danya was still grieving the loss of his son. After what she'd been through, she could certainly understand his pain and desire to keep his only other son left close by.

Senetra started the chore of cleaning up the kitchen and then her bedroom before she wiped down the bathroom again. She'd call Kathryn later and make plans.

George Avery was getting a cup of coffee at six when Colin Mayes came tearing in.

"Breakfast ready?" the younger man asked. "Sure smells like it."

Colin was George's granddaughter's husband and his late partner's grandson. They'd worked together even before George was aware he had grandchildren.

"Mrs. Jackson up yet?" Colin asked.

"Yes. She'll be in soon."

"Well, I'm going to eat and—"

"We'll wait for Dorothelia," George said in a firm voice.

"But—"

"We'll wait," George said with a finality that had the younger man stopping. "Both of us."

George knew Colin wanted to ask questions, but George opened his paper, closing off any opportunity for discussion or argument. Dorothelia was his guest. He did not have to make excuses in his own home.

Colin sipped his coffee, leaned over the table and grabbed the sports section. Then with great exaggeration, he sniffed the air. "Is that cologne I smell?"

George felt like squirming, but curtailed the impulse. "Must be the new soap Leila bought," George said as he turned a page of his paper. A glimpse over the top revealed a grinning Colin. The impudent scamp.

"So, we have a courtship going on here. No wonder you're all decked out. I hope it doesn't confuse the horses."

"Mind your business, young man."

"Good morning," Dorothelia said in her sweet, melodious voice, looking quite pretty in her blue slacks and colorful blouse. She smelled delightful, too. "I hope I didn't keep you waiting."

"Not at all." George set his paper aside and stood.

"I just walked in," Colin said. "You look very lovely, Mrs. Jackson."

"Why, thank you, Colin."

Jasmine, George's other granddaughter, and her husband, Drake Whitcomb, came in looking as if someone had just yanked them from the bed. George shook his head. Jasmine dragged her hand through her short hair and spoke.

"Breakfast is ready," George said. The couple usually slept in on Saturdays if they weren't on call. He felt a little guilty getting them up so early, as they were both veterinarians and worked long hours, but it was the first morning he could get them all together. He wanted Dorothelia to feel comfortable around his family.

Colin extended his arm for Dorothelia to take. "May I escort you to the table?"

She blushed as she put her hands in his. "Why, thank you."

Colin grinned at George's thunderous expression before leading Mrs. Jackson to the table.

That boy needs to be taken down a peg, George thought, following them, miffed at having the opportunity to touch Dorothelia's soft skin thwarted. As they passed by, he caught a whiff of Dorothelia's pleasing perfume and his mood lightened.

"Have you heard anything from the private investigator yet?" Dorothelia asked as she spread her napkin in her lap.

"Nothing yet," George said. "But the agency is very good. It's only been a week."

"I guess I'm just too nervous. I should be getting back to Los Angeles."

"We could hear something any day. Then you and I will fly out to see her. You don't have any pressing business back home, do you?"

"Well…I don't want to be an imposition. I'm sure you have plenty of work to do."

"You aren't an imposition at all. Think nothing of it, dear."

"We really love having you here, Mrs. Jackson," Colin said. "Look at this place. An entire platoon could stay here and wouldn't make a ripple. Unfortunately, we're gone most of the day. I wish we could spend more time with you."

"I don't need to be entertained," Dorothelia said. "Think nothing of it. I think it's a wonderful place."

"Then please feel at home here. This is Senetra's home, too, even though she doesn't know it yet," George said.

"Thank you. You're so kind." She dished food onto her plate and George was pleased she'd be here a little longer, though he wished he could wipe the sadness from her eyes. He was going to spend the day with her, at least. Perhaps he'd invite her to the Kentucky Derby. They had a horse racing there this year.

George dished pancakes onto his plate. He hadn't felt attraction to a woman like this since his dear wife passed away. He never thought he'd feel this way again. And yet... He stifled a sigh. The Lord was certainly good to him. He'd lost his dear son and wife, but now he had three grandchildren and a new woman he was very attracted to. How could life get any better? There wasn't a doubt in his mind that he'd find Senetra. He just wished they were quicker about doing it.

"Did she ever talk about places she wanted to visit?" Drake asked.

"I mentioned all of them to the investigator. She likes warm climates."

"If it was me, I'd go to a place he'd never think to look," Jasmine said, and all eyes veered to her. "Well, I would. Why go someplace he'd automatically search?"

"She hates the cold weather," Dorothelia said slowly. "It's what she disliked most about Wisconsin."

"North Dakota or Montana," Jasmine said. "I wouldn't even consider Florida or Texas. Forget South Carolina or Georgia."

"Blacks would stick out like sore thumbs in North Dakota or Montana," Colin offered.

"He wouldn't search there, so what? There are a million places in this country where there are only a handful of us he'd never think she'd go to."

"She could be in some remote location in Nevada or Arizona. Like the high desert where it gets cold but not like Wisconsin or Montana," Drake murmured.

"Nome, Alaska. She's not going near the desert," Jasmine said. "Even I could find her in Nevada. Besides, she's learned to live with the cold in Wisconsin. At least this way, she might have to sit in front of a roaring fire, but she's free. If nothing else, she can hibernate until the spring thaw."

"Make that summer," Drake said.

"You've got a point," George mused. "I'll call the investigator after breakfast."

After breakfast everyone scattered in different directions. Colin and George went out to the barn to deal with a problem with one of the stallions.

George had asked Dorothelia if she would like to go into D.C. to look at the cherry blossoms even though it was still a little early in the season. They'd had a mild winter and the trees were blooming already.

Dorothelia agreed. She was somewhat flustered. George was so different from the men she usually met—

very handsome and such a gentleman. But most of all,
his kindness touched her. Long ago, she'd given up on
ever finding someone to share an intimate relationship
with. But George seemed as attracted to her as she was
to him. And she felt guilty because she should be con-
centrating on her daughter, not Senetra's grandfather.

She might be in her midsixties, but she was still a
woman and had a woman's needs.

It was odd having nothing to do. But at nine-thirty
the mail arrived and with it a package for her. She'd
asked her friend to pick up her mail once a week and
send it to her.

Sitting on the comfortable sofa in her suite, she
opened her mail. There were several letters and enough
junk mail to outfit a tree. But there was also a letter
from Senetra. Dorothelia's heart gladdened. Did she
know about Timothy?

With bated breath, Dorothelia tore into the letter to
read it first.

She sighed with disappointment and frustration. She
didn't know about Timothy, but on the other hand she'd
had a wonderful birthday. Something to be pleased
about.

"Oh, darling. I wish I knew where you were." Tears
came to Dorothelia's eyes. She missed Senetra so
much.

A knock on her door brought her up from the sofa,
wiping her eyes.

It was George.

"What's wrong?" he asked with concern.

She still clutched the letter in her hand. She handed

it to George. "I got a letter from Senetra in the mail today."

"Do you mind if I read it?"

"Please do."

George glanced at the envelope first. "It's postmarked from Los Angeles."

"They all are. From the same postal area."

"Do you know who might be mailing them?"

"I don't think it's anyone she knows. I think it's being mailed to someone she might know in another location in the country and that person mails it to someone Senetra doesn't even know. I know she set up an intricate network before she left."

"Smart girl."

"A little too smart," Dorothelia said with a wry glance. "Which makes it very difficult to find her."

George stroked her arm. "We will find her."

A tear slipped from Dorothelia's eye and George gently wiped it away and held her in his arms.

She'd shouldered her burdens alone for so long. It was so nice to be able to share this with someone. Not that she discounted her very good friends back home. Rachel especially had been a lifeline to her.

Dorothelia was unaware of when the moment turned from gentle comfort to desire. But suddenly they were looking at each other. Her hand was pressed against his strong chest and he held her gently in his arms, but the desire in his eyes was unmistakable.

"If you don't want me to kiss you, speak up quickly," George said.

Dorothelia bit her bottom lip. "And if I do, shall I remain silent?"

The shift of emotions in his eyes was telling. And as his head lowered, hers tilted toward him. It was Dorothelia's first kiss in many years and the hunger hit her hard. And when his mouth touched hers, her heart thudded against her breast.

One of his hands rested against her back, the other against her cheek. Desire and need raged in her as what started out as a soft and gentle kiss turned hot and demanding.

George kissed with a skill and an emotion that was breath stealing.

They heard a noise, a quickly indrawn breath and hurried footsteps leaving the area.

They came apart like teenagers caught necking in the broom closet.

"Well," George said around a chuckle. "It's been many years since I've lost my head so completely."

Dorothelia laughed, too.

"Are you ready to leave, my dear?" George said softly, but he still held her within the circle of his arms and it felt so good.

Still riding on a cloud of desire, Dorothelia nodded.

Dorothelia hoped Senetra was experiencing a new love, too. That a new and wonderful experience was in the offing for them both.

Chapter 7

A host of activities was going on at the Spit. A brisk wind blew over the area. Children drank hot chocolate and adults drank hot coffee to keep warm. Kathryn and Senetra stood hovering in the cold, sipping on cups of piping-hot coffee, talking with the locals while they waited for Rick and Alex to return. Several boats had already pulled up to the dock. Many of the fishermen appeared to be immune to the cold. And Senetra guessed they were, since they fished in weather much more frigid.

Salmon was weighed and smaller prizes were given out on the hour.

Food stands did record business selling their succulent and delicious fare. Senetra ate fried clams and meandered closer to the scales where a crowd gathered.

She had a few more shots left in her camera and took pictures of some of her students who participated.

"So, tell me. How are things with Alex?" Kathryn asked with a sly smile. "I heard he spent the night."

"I was a little upset after the altercation with Danya. He didn't want to leave me alone, that's all. So don't try to make it into more than it was."

"Am I getting a false impression? Because you're out here waiting for him to come back."

"I'm taking shots of my students." She narrowed her gaze. "And waiting for Alex. Okay, okay. I like him."

"You say it as if there's something wrong with liking him."

"I don't know if I'm ready."

"You don't have to marry him, Regina. But I think he really likes you."

Senetra contemplated a moment. She usually kept her thoughts to herself. Kathryn was her friend, had been from the moment she moved there. Maybe it was time to trust her—to a certain point anyway.

"My last relationship wasn't good, Kat. I don't want to rush things. I just want to take this slowly. I'm leery of getting in over my head again. And that's easy to do if I move too quickly with the heat of the moment."

Kathryn brushed Senetra's hair out of her face and smiled sadly. "Oh, honey. I knew it was something. I could tell there were demons from the moment I met you. And I know you've lived cautiously because of your past," she said. "I just... You can't give the one who hurt you that kind of power over you. The power to steal the joy you can experience with other men, even if it doesn't work out with Alex. There's going to be someone you eventually fall for."

"I know, but..."

"You like Alex enough to give it a try, don't you?" Kathryn asked with a hopeful expression.

Senetra nodded.

"You both take life so seriously. You should talk about his past. He's had his share of pain, too. And sometimes like souls draw together, they can be comfort for each other."

"Was it just another woman?" She already knew about Jessica, but was there more?

"I'm going to let him tell you. He's not secretive. But he's taking things cautiously with you. He's as afraid of getting hurt as you are."

"Or he's still in love with another woman. I don't exactly want a rebound situation, either."

"Trust me. Alex wouldn't waste time with you if it wasn't real. He's not that kind of guy."

They linked arms and walked closer to an open fire pit to warm up.

"I think I see them in the distance," Kathryn said, shading her eyes with her hand.

"Which one? Looks like a million boats are out there. How can you tell one from the other at this distance?" she asked, searching, but couldn't find anything distinctive enough. "Anyway, it's three-thirty. You know very well Rick isn't coming in before he absolutely has to. There were over four hundred boats in the tournament last year."

"Let's hope someone convinced him to come in early."

"It's too bad you don't like to fish," Senetra said. "Then the two of you would be quite a team."

"If fishing is the defining factor on us being a team, we won't make it. I won't go out on a cold, blustery morning fishing when I can snuggle up under my warm comforter, and I don't clean fish."

Senetra laughed.

"They're here," Kathryn said, waving enthusiastically as the boat drew to the dock.

The two of them ran toward the boat.

Four of the guys were on deck, looking cold yet happy as they carted their fish to the scales. Senetra snapped a couple of pictures.

"Wonder how much they've been drinking?" Senetra asked. The guys looked dizzy on adrenaline.

"Not much yet, but tonight's a different story."

As their salmon was being weighed, Senetra snapped off more shots. She took a perfect one of Alex alone with the huge fish. She planned to frame a copy of it for him.

Among the hustle and bustle, the fish was weighed. They won in their category—one thousand dollars split among the six men.

"A big party to celebrate," they said, "but the winning captain's throwing a party at the Pit." They were all meeting there later. The finalist won nearly fifty grand, but it wasn't the money as much as the sport of it that brought the men out in droves each year. As low-key as Alex was, she could tell he enjoyed himself.

"I smell pretty rank so I won't get too close," he said with a twisted grin. "But could the winner get just a little kiss?" he asked with a boyish grin.

"Sure." Despite the ripe scent of eau de fish, she felt a pleasant jolt to her system when she kissed him.

"Ah," he moaned, and shook his head, smacking his lips facetiously. "That made it all worthwhile. Where can I sign up again for next year?"

Senetra laughed.

Alex went to Rick's place to clean up before he picked Senetra up. It was six when Alex and Senetra walked into the bar. The music was loud and beer and other drinks were liberally enjoyed. It felt as if a thousand fishermen had shown up, but the only man on Senetra's mind was Alex.

He'd cleaned up nicely for the occasion. He wore another cable-knit sweater—black this time—and Senetra was really turned on all over again.

The crush of people in the bar pushed Senetra up against Alex. He inhaled a deep breath to keep his libido intact. He thought he'd never love another woman the way he'd loved Jessica, but right now what he'd felt in the past paled in comparison to what he felt that moment. He didn't know if it was mere sex or what, but it was strong and intense. Whatever it was, he was in for the ride. Yet he had to remember she was still skittish about being in a relationship.

Alex pulled her close in his arms. Her body molded perfectly to his.

"Are you going to let me stay the night?" he asked. "Or do I have to camp out on Rick's sofa?"

She threw him a wary glance before she looked away. "I'm not quite ready," she said.

"Okay." He pulled her closer. "At least I get to hold you now," he said, trying to control the desire waging a war in his body.

His phone buzzed against them.

"What's that?"

"My cell." Alex pulled it out and glanced at the number. "My dad. I have to take this. Be right back."

The phone had stopped ringing by the time Alex answered it. He called his father back and the older man picked up on the first ring.

"What's up, Dad?"

"It's all settled. All your sisters and brothers are coming for Easter. They're spending the week here and they're all looking forward to seeing you," he said. "You are coming, aren't you?"

Alex stifled a groan. His dad was trying so hard to mend the rift between him and his siblings. "I had planned to stay in Alaska."

"You haven't been home for more than a day or so in two years. You get some vacation time."

Alex sighed. He'd planned to visit Senetra again. Things were going pretty good with them and he didn't want to give her too much time alone—without him.

"When will you get here?" his father asked as if his silence was agreement. "The whole family plans to attend Easter service together. Be good having everyone home at the same time for a change."

With no other option, Alex knew he had to give in. His father was right. It was time to go home. He only wished he could take Senetra with him, but that wasn't going to happen. She didn't trust him enough, and if she was in hiding she was risking danger.

"I'll call and let you know when I'll arrive," Alex finally said.

Besides, he couldn't put the confrontation with his siblings off forever. He might as well get it over with once and for all. It would be good to see his nieces and nephews. A couple of his nephews had visited him last summer. One had just graduated from high school and the trip was a graduation present from Alex. Alex had taken some time off to show him around. He'd really enjoyed it.

"Okay, I'll see you soon," his father said, and hung up.

Alex closed his phone and breathed in the brisk, cold air. As much as he desired Senetra, he was unsure how he would react once he saw Jessica again. His desire for Senetra was sharp and real. But it was time for him to face the demons of his past. All of them. His siblings and Jessica. It was also time for him to move forward.

He returned to the party and found Senetra sitting at their table, nursing a ginger ale. Rick and Kathryn were talking to someone near the pool table.

She smiled when she saw him. "Is everything okay at home?"

"Just fine. My father has been hassling me about coming home for Easter. I finally gave in."

"Good," she said with a wistfulness that let him know she longed for home, too.

"Are you going home for the break?" he asked since he wasn't supposed to know who she was.

Senetra looked down and sadness sapped the gaiety of the moment. "No."

Alex wished he'd kept his mouth shut.

Alex knew he had to ease his way into Senetra's life with simple measures. Do small things with a big impact to make memorable impressions.

Alex took Senetra home around twelve. They sat in front of the fire and talked for a couple of hours over steaming cups of hot chocolate.

"Have you ever gone clamming?" he asked.

She laughed. "No. I buy mine from the dock. As a matter of fact, I'm going to buy some tomorrow for clam chowder."

"Let's go clamming instead. Rick has everything we need. We'll go around eight. The ground should be soft enough, and it shouldn't take long. You're in Alaska, woman. You may as well experience all of it."

Senetra laughed, and it sounded like sweet music to Alex's soul. "You really want to go clamming?" she asked skeptically.

As long as it's with you, Alex thought, although he'd much prefer spending his morning in bed with her. But this was a good way to work his way there. He still couldn't get the night of the hot tub out of his mind. How soft she felt. He had dreams about her. But he merely nodded. Clambering around in the mud would certainly take his mind off sex.

"Okay," she said uncertainly. Her expression was just as dubious as his. But what else were they going to do? Alex wondered. He couldn't take much more of this chaste stuff or sitting in her cozy apartment making small talk. He needed to do something to expend energy, especially if he couldn't get her into bed.

"Guess I should be going," he said.

It was two in the morning and Senetra was surprised that she didn't want him to go. She almost regretted that she told him he couldn't spend the night. Before she could complete the thought, Alex weaved his hand through her hair, pulled her closer to him and lowered his lips to hers. He tasted sweet from the cocoa and whipped cream. She moaned. She wouldn't think of the things one could do with whipped cream. His first kiss was gentle. His tongue traced the soft fullness of her lips.

Like the beginning of the kiss the night under the stars, the sweetness of it set her aflame. Now, like then, he gently sucked on her bottom lip and then thrust his tongue into her mouth, caressing the roof, dueling with her tongue, enjoying the mating dance. Her breasts tingled. And the butterflies in her stomach were doing a pas de deux. Her heartbeat quickened as new spirals of ecstasy exploded through her.

She wanted, needed more. She felt his arm move slowly down her arm, his touch lighting a deeper fire until he touched her breasts. She gasped with a need so intense she nearly cried out. The hot sensation flashing through her had her digging her fingers in his strong shoulders. She was not surprised by her own sharp response to his touch.

This kissing and nothing else was driving Alex slowly insane. Alex couldn't stand it. He had to get out or he'd be in agony for the rest of the night. He already was in agony. Courting Senetra slowly was killing him.

He pressed his fingers through the silky strands of hair and pulled away from her. His heartbeat thundered in his chest. He inhaled deeply. "I've got to go, baby."

Without fanfare, Alex stood and blew out a long frustrated breath. She looked wide-eyed at him as if she wanted him as much as he desired her. Alex briefly closed his eyes, willing his hands not to reach for her again. He ran a shaky hand across his forehead and looked at her again.

"I haven't gone this slowly since high school. You must be good for me, even if you're not good *to* me. But we'll take things at your speed. Only, don't take too long, baby. Or I'm going to go completely out of my mind."

Senetra laughed. "Not fair. I'm good to you."

He moaned, his body still fighting his desire. He wouldn't even dignify that with a response. He headed to her closet for his coat and shrugged into it, although the heat coming from him was enough to keep him warm.

"I'll pick you up at five of eight."

"Okay."

He tapped her on the nose. "Dress warmly."

"I will."

Senetra closed the door after him, and leaning against the surface, she recalled her conversation with Kathryn.

Her body was humming with need. She moaned. She was torturing both of them, but what she said was true. She didn't really know Alex and she didn't want to rush into anything. Oh, crap. Maybe she was just too cautious. Maybe she should just throw her inhibitions to the wind and enjoy herself.

If she'd done that, she'd be in bed with Alex right this moment instead of going to bed with this driving hunger.

She wanted this relationship to be different from what she'd had with Timothy. And Alex *was* different. Everything was different. They weren't rushing into everything. They didn't fall in love at first sight.

Okay, things had gotten out of hand the very first day. That wasn't using caution at all. But she was making up for that. Or was she overcompensating?

After a day of fishing, Alex didn't exactly want to go wading in the mud digging for clams on his last day with Senetra, but it was exactly what he did with boots reaching his knees and buckled up in Rick's oldest coat. No, he'd much rather spend the day in bed with Senetra. But that wasn't going to happen. No sense in getting his hopes up.

Alex gave Senetra his share of the salmon filets before they left.

"So, where are the best places to dig?" Alex asked.

Senetra glanced at him. "I thought you knew."

"You live here."

"But I don't go clamming. I buy them from the store like most people."

Alex looked skyward. "Nobody in Alaska stays shut up in the house when there's so much to do."

"I do."

"Right." He gave her a long look. He didn't want her to close up on him. "That's going to change." He was optimistic when she didn't show fear or tell him to mind his own business. He picked up her hand and kissed the back, then drove a short distance by the water to one of the many clam beds at the shore. A few people were already out there, their children and dogs romping in the mud, dogs barking and running around like crazy.

The air was so cold the vapor from their breaths clouded as they spoke.

"Whose idea was this?" Alex drawled with self-mockery.

"Definitely your idea," Senetra mumbled with a shiver. "I wouldn't have suggested anything so crazy on a Sunday morning."

"A great substitution for scx." It was the first time he'd come out and said it, and Senetra blushed.

"The cold should cool your ardor in no time."

Senetra's boots hiked up to her thighs. It seemed to become even colder as they slushed about in the mud-flats with shovel, rubber gloves and a bucket.

"It's not working. I'm still thinking about sex," Alex said.

Senetra laughed. "Typical male."

"What do you expect? I've already felt you," he said with a wicked gleam in his eye. "And it was great."

"Think clams and church."

His eyebrow quirked. "You're kidding, right?"

"I've just discovered you have a one-track mind."

"I work with a bunch of guys. I can't help it."

"Think clams."

As if that was going to work. Alex sighed. It took no time to find their first dimple.

"Can you tell the difference between the dimples that indicate worms from the ones that signal clams?" Senetra asked.

"Of course. One is right here," he said with authority, burrowing the shovel in and digging deep. Falling to his knees, Alex slipped his hand in and pulled the first one up. "Ta-da. Beginner's luck."

"We'll have clam chowder for lunch after all," Senetra said, holding out the bucket. "And what's this about beginners? I thought you were an old hand."

"A few times with Rick."

She stood there, holding the bucket while he dug a few holes.

"You don't get to just hold the bucket and look pretty," Alex muttered. "You're going to get down and dirty, too. No sense in me having all the fun."

Senetra rolled her eyes skyward, but she was game. "Oh, so you love to share. I'm learning something new about you every day."

"I'm good at sharing," he said, tapping her on the nose with a muddy finger.

A couple of hours later, they had enough clams to

fry and for several batches of soup. By then more dogs and kids were romping on the beach while their parents did some serious digging. Some of the kids pitched in, too. It was just another game to the younger ones.

Alex had put newspaper on the floor of the car to keep it from getting too dirty with their mud-caked boots.

Senetra held her hands up. "Bet you don't want to kiss my hands now," she said.

Alex came close, slowly leaned into her, giving her plenty of opportunity to move away if she wanted to. She didn't want to. And he kissed her, driving his tongue into her warm mouth, a stark contrast to her cold lips.

"I've enjoyed this weekend," she said softly when their lips parted.

"It's not over yet," Alex murmured with a definite wicked look, and opened the door to put the clam bucket in the back.

Senetra grabbed a breath to calm herself as Alex got into the car. The feelings exploding through her were confusing and wonderful.

When they got back to the apartment, they heated water and cleaned the clams, exposing the perfectly white filets.

Senetra prepared a big pot of soup and went to take a shower. "I'm going to send half of this soup with you, if you can take food back?"

"I've got a woman who can cook. And this soup is so good. I'll take as much as you can give me."

"You guys make such a big deal over that."

"Doggone right. Women today don't cook the way they used to."

"With careers being what they are, it's no wonder."

Alex went to Rick's apartment to shower and change, leaving some of the clams for him.

Later, while Senetra coated some clams with an egg mixture and cracker meal before frying them, Alex made a fire in the fireplace. They ate their meal of chowder and fried clams in front of the blazing flames.

"I've died and gone to heaven, even if I did cook it. I love the fresh seafood in this place," she said.

"Yeah, me, too."

She pushed her plate aside. "So tell me, how did a guy from Wisconsin make it to the wilds of Alaska? I realize you're an engineer, but I'd think you'd want to settle closer to home, be near family."

"I did. But my father was in a terrible farming accident a couple of years ago and had let his health insurance lapse. He needed extensive surgery," Alex said, stretching out his legs. "He would have had to sell the farm to get any help. I was able to make enough money here to pay for everything. I made the last payment a couple months ago."

"Alex. That was so selfless of you."

"He's my dad. My parents have always done their best by us. But my siblings and I had a huge fight before I left. My dad insisted on selling a few acres of the family land to pay for the expenses. When I found out that he was selling for substantially less than the land was worth, I renegotiated the deal. My siblings resented the fact that I let him sell it at all. But he insisted. There was nothing I could do but keep him from selling more. They resented the fact that I took matters in my own hands." Alex glared up at the ceiling. "But they're all married. Most of them have children, a couple in college. I had the least to lose, so I did what I thought I should do."

"They should be thankful."

"We've barely spoken in two years."

"I'm sorry."

Alex shrugged.

"So now that you've paid off your father's debt, are you going home soon?"

"Not for at least another two years. I'm under contract and would like to fulfill my obligation. Also, my dad is sixty-five now and has Medicare, as well as insurance, so at least that's taken care of.

"So how do you like it here? What brought you here?" He chuckled. "Especially since you don't like the out-of-doors."

"I like the small-community feel of this place. It's a slower pace than most cities and it has modern conveniences—hospitals, cultural activities."

"How long do you plan to stay?"

"It's my home. I'm not leaving."

There was sadness in her voice as if her stay wasn't a choice. Alex wondered if she missed Timothy. Even though it was obvious her husband had been abusive, did she long to go back to recapture the love of their relationship?

Even knowing this might not be the right move, that

she might not be ready to move on, he was going to test the waters. He leaned close and pressed his lips to hers. If she didn't want his advances, she could easily push him away and he'd back off. But he longed to be close to her.

And then her tongue dueled with his, sucking the very breath out of him. His arms closed completely around her, pulling her close into him. He forgot about the past, hers and his. All he wanted at this very moment was to drive himself completely inside her. But he took their lovemaking slowly. He smoothed kisses over her cheek, neck, collarbone, shifting her sweater aside to taste the sweet, sweet texture of her soft breasts.

She tasted like ambrosia.

"Regina, I want to make love with you, but I don't want to rush you if you aren't ready."

If he'd been more demanding, Senetra would have declined immediately. But he'd been thoughtful. Gentle. He'd followed her lead, but the desire she saw in his eyes matched her own need. Biting her lip, Senetra whispered, "I want you, too."

Alex leaned back. "Do you mean that? I'm not rushing you?"

Senetra bit her bottom lip and gazed directly at him. "Yes and no. I mean it and I'm ready for you, too," she said softly.

She did not have to explain or repeat herself. He lifted her from the sofa and headed in the only direction that could lead to her bedroom. He took a cursory glance around the spacious area and placed her in the center of a white comforter topped with a thousand colorful pillows, brushing them aside with his arm. Many candles were on top of the dresser.

Very feminine, he thought as he caught a light whiff of flowers and a fireplace that looked as if she used it often.

"We should have started a fire in here," he said. "But I can't go another moment without you."

"You've already lit a fire in me," Senetra said, and Alex grabbed for breath, for calm when he wanted to unleash all the pent-up desire that had raged for Senetra for two long weeks. From the first moment he'd touched her, he'd constructed all kinds of fantasies around her. But he wanted this to be great for her, and memorable.

So he started out slowly, kissed her until he knew the texture of her face, the taste of her mouth, the silky delicious taste of her skin.

One by one, he peeled clothes from her heated body and rewarded each area with sweet kisses.

But Senetra wasn't idle. She tugged at Alex's clothes, pulling them off until his entire magnificent body was revealed to her. She took a moment to look at him. When she'd thought of him during the last two weeks, she thought her imagination was adding to what was there, but now she knew he was even better.

"You're beautiful," she whispered, tracing her fingers down the length of his chest.

His chuckle was deep. "I've never been described quite that way before." He nipped her thigh and then soothed it with his tongue.

She moaned, pressing her fingers into his shoulders.

He stroked her breasts with his tongue, then tugged gently on one nipple and then the other, shooting sparks of pleasure to her center. The pleasure was so intense she screamed out loud.

"You like that, baby?" he asked, his face tense with desire and need.

"Yes," exploded from her.

While she touched places that drove him nearly out of his mind, his tongue wove a path between her breasts, down her ribs to her stomach.

Whether his touch was more defined or lightly teasing, he found every pleasure point. When she could stand it no more, he paused to kiss her, whispering his love for every part of her body.

He grabbed his pants, dug into his pocket for a condom, dropping it on her. She ripped the package open and slid it on him, stoking him while he groaned his pleasure.

And then he entered her, stretching her wide and filling her completely.

They both released moans of delight.

Love flowed in Senetra like warm honey.

Their bodies moved in exquisite harmony, drawing her to new heights of pleasure she'd never experienced before.

He moved his hand under her bottom, sinking deeper into her. The pleasure increased to higher levels of ecstasy until her world was filled with him.

Senetra had expected to fake an orgasm, but bliss arced through her until her thoughts fragmented as she went over the edge. She screamed her fulfillment and savored the feeling of satisfaction he left her with.

Later, they lay together spoon fashion, gazing out the window, with Senetra in front of him. It was snowing. She turned to face him.

"That's never happened before," she said.

"What?"

"An orgasm while making love," she said shyly.

He brushed her hair from her face. "I wouldn't have come before you. Your pleasure means everything, Regina. It's not fair and real if both of us don't receive pleasure from our lovemaking."

She walked her fingers up his chest. "Trust me," she said, kissing his amazing chest. "I was quite pleased. But I'm curious," she murmured.

"What about?"

"The night in the hot tub. You dropped me like a hot potato as if you hated the fact that you'd touched me."

His eyes flickered. "I hadn't meant to. It was obvious you didn't want to be saddled with me."

She searched his face. "For some reason I thought it was more than that."

"I'd just heard Jessica was pregnant. I wasn't completely over that."

"And now?" Senetra rubbed his arm.

"Jessica is part of my past. You're my present and I'm satisfied with this new and exciting relationship with you." He kissed her nose, but Senetra wasn't convinced he was completely over Jessica yet.

She had to be careful with her heart. Rebound situations could be tricky.

Senetra stood at the bay, waiting for Alex's plane to take off for Anchorage. She wished he could stay longer and so did he.

"Here's my number," he said, handing her a card. "Both my cell and my office numbers and e-mail. If you need me for anything—absolutely anything—call me." He wrapped a hand around the side of her neck. "This is special, what we have."

"I—"

"It is. I know what I feel when I'm with you. And it's special."

"You don't know me at all," Senetra said, wondering what he'd really feel about a woman who let herself be victimized the way she had. Who'd let herself be completely taken over by another person. She knew it started with a systematic attack on her self-esteem. But when a person hadn't experienced it, he didn't quite see it that way.

"I know what counts." It was time for him to board the plane. "I'll call you." He smiled. "You're going to get tired of hearing from me."

Senetra smiled, too. "I doubt it."

"When do you get out for the summer?"

"The middle of June."

"Send me an e-mail of the exact date. I'll take that week off," he said, "if you'll spend it with me. We can tour the islands together. We'll take the southwest route to Unalaska and Dutch Harbor with stops at Kodiak,

Port Lions, Chignik, Sand Point and a few more places. It's absolutely beautiful. We'll see the active volcanoes, birds and wildlife like seals and walruses. I'll book a stateroom and rent a four-wheel-drive. Some of the roads are pretty treacherous, so you don't want to use your own vehicle."

"That sounds wonderful, but let's wait and see. We've got time."

"We'll talk about it. It's a wonderful tour. You'll have a great time. I promise."

"I—"

He touched her lips. "Just think about it."

People were beginning to board the plane.

"I have to go." They both got out of the SUV. He pulled her close and kissed her deeply one last time as if he didn't want to let her go. "I'll call." And then he was walking aboard.

Once he disappeared, Senetra watched until the plane took off. She felt as if she'd lived a year in one weekend.

Chapter 8

Spring break was coming soon, Senetra thought as she gathered mail from her box. Many of her friends were taking trips to warmer climates or participating in some family activity in the area. Even Kathryn was planning a trip with Rick. But Senetra made no plans. Would the rest of her life be this way? Time would pass by, but she'd stay hidden and hovering in this quiet little town. True, she liked the area, but she'd planned to see other places, to see the world.

The idea of taking the trip with Alex when school closed was tempting. She weighed the pros and cons. She was comfortable with Alex. But the locations would take her away from her escape route, her sense of safety.

Besides, she'd always wanted to tour other places in Alaska and wasn't likely to do so alone. At the sites he'd mentioned, she probably wouldn't see anyone from her past. She laughed. No indeed. Not even Timothy would don rugged wear and tramp around in the tall grass with binoculars to watch caribou, bears and birds.

If it wasn't a political engagement or a suit-and-tie affair, Timothy wouldn't be interested.

"Trying to solve the problems of the world?" Kathryn said, coming up beside her.

"Not exactly. Alex wants to go away with me at the end of the school year."

"To where?" she asked, and Senetra told her.

"And you're actually considering going?" Kathryn asked, clearly surprised, yet pleased. "My God, I thought I'd have to tie you up for your birthday weekend. You've come a long way, girl."

Senetra moaned. "I wasn't that bad."

"He's had a good effect on you. I couldn't believe it when he woke us up at seven telling us he was taking you clamming. I just couldn't picture you digging in the mud, much less pulling slippery clams out of it, or did you just hold the bucket? You're always so put together, you know. *I'll* go digging in the mud, but not you."

"I'm open for new challenges," Senetra assured her.

Kathryn gave her a droll look. "This is Kat you're talking to, kiddo. When you first came here, a stroll down to the Spit was a big deal for you. We're a couple of blocks away. I couldn't believe you actually drove there at first."

Senetra stuck her nose in the air. "There are bears all around. Of course I drove there."

Kathryn laughed. "You act as if you need a getaway car everywhere you go."

Kathryn didn't know it, but she wasn't far from the truth. But she wondered if others shared the same impression. "Was I that bad?"

Kathryn nodded. "Yeah. But that's okay. You're not snobbish, just reserved. And I can live with that. Sometimes I come on a little too strong."

"I think I needed that. Thanks for being my friend."

She hugged Kathryn.

"Oh, Reg. You're my friend, too," Kathryn said.

"So what are you doing for the break?"

"Rick wants to do some hiking, but I want a more relaxing vacation where we can do some of the things I like for a change. A spa or lie out on a beach. Rick can go fishing in Hawaii, but sometimes I wish we could just spend the day together without me feeling like I have to compete in a sport."

"Have you told him how you feel?"

"Sure I do, but when Rick starts planning, he hears only what he wants to. He's even thinking of moving to a more remote location in Alaska. Somewhere farther north, but I don't want to leave here," Kathryn said. "I like it for the same reason you do. It's remote enough, but with plenty to do and with cultural activities. I don't want to live in an area without modern conveniences. I want to buy a house here." Kathryn emitted a long sigh. "I'm just so frustrated. We've dated for two years now, and I don't think we're getting any closer to settling down."

"Tell you the truth, settling down here sounds ideal to me, too," Senetra said.

"You think Alex will want to stay here forever?"

"I just met Alex. I can't plan my future around him. He may have other plans."

Kathryn shook her head. "You never can tell about people. I can see you snuggled down with husband and children, directing every facet of their lives. He'd have to introduce them to more adventurous pursuits, but I can see you trotting them to piano lessons and ballet classes. Hubby would have to do the skiing and fishing."

Had she changed that much? "Ah, bliss."

They reached Senetra's apartment. She opened the door and both of them went in.

"For some. I wanted to explore the world before I settled down, but I never expected to be single forever. I'm twenty-eight," Kathryn murmured. "I've done many of the things I've wanted to do."

"I've just begun." She'd had dreams, too. She'd thought she and Timothy could one day travel and enjoy the world together. In her dreams, Alaska was a cruise and side trips, not where she lived or took weeklong trips roughing it. But she'd enjoyed clamming with Alex. And on her birthday weekend, a time when she'd thought she'd celebrate it swamped in nostalgia and missing her mother, she'd enjoyed the B and B, walking on the glacier and skiing with her friends and Alex. Most of all, she'd enjoyed being snuggled up in his arms.

She had no doubt she'd enjoy their week's adventure on the ferry. She was going to do it. She wondered if she'd ever trust him enough to tell him about her past.

"I may as well go. I'll pick you up at nine for the bar."

"Okay," Senetra said, missing Alex already.

Alex left work and made his way to his room, wondering if he really was going to make it two more years there. Most guys had pictures of loved ones on their bedside tables, but not him. Sensing her reticence, he hadn't asked Senetra for one.

He'd called Senetra practically every night. He was trying not to make a pest of himself, but he found himself dialing her number. The last two years hadn't been so bad. He didn't really have anything to go back home to, but now...

He smiled when he heard Senetra's sweet voice. "Going to the Pit tonight?" he asked.

"I let Kat talk me into it. What about you? What do you do for fun there?"

"They have a game room. Movie night. I'll probably just watch a movie in my room, or I might play cards or shoot pool. Who knows?"

"Oh, well, I won't be out long. But the Pit is better than vegging out in my apartment."

"So, what's happening with the husky?"

"Nothing for now. I'm considering buying a house in another year. I'll get a dog then."

They were talking about inconsequential things, but he just wanted to hear her voice.

They talked a few more minutes and Senetra left for the bar. Rick was already there playing poker in one of the rooms. Senetra had considered driving since more than likely she'd leave earlier and Kathryn would leave with Rick, but she could always take a cab.

They sat at the table with Iris and some of the other ladies.

"She let Danya move back in," someone informed them.

Senetra cocked an eyebrow. "Really?"

"Ah, the big ox is plenty warm on cold nights," Iris said in her own defense.

"I bet he is," Kathryn mumbled.

"But I bet he makes her hot in other ways, too," someone teased, and Iris blushed.

Senetra ordered a beer and later left to play a game of pool, but she was ready to leave around eleven.

"I'll take you home," Kathryn said.

"Don't bother. I'll take a cab. Stay and enjoy yourself."

Back at her apartment, Senetra started her cozy fire. The last time they'd spoken, Alex had teased her about her love for fires. She got out his card, scraping it against the edge of her thumb. On it was an address. She could write him a letter and send a small gift, but what? If circumstances were normal, she could send a picture of the two of them, but she couldn't give him a picture of her. She could give him a picture she took on her birthday weekend. There were plenty of him alone and with Rick and Kathryn.

Senetra pulled out her digital camera and a note card. She wrote a short letter and printed off a picture of him standing beside the huge king salmon they'd caught. His father would love that. Probably brag about it with his friends.

In high school she would have spritzed on some perfume, but not now. Sealing the envelope, she placed a stamp and return address on it.

She wrote her mother a much longer letter, even told her about Alex, although she omitted his name. She made sure to add that his personality was completely the opposite of Timothy's and why. And the reason he'd changed jobs. It would show character and that would please her mother. She wanted her mother to know she was moving on with her life. Maybe Dorothelia wouldn't worry so much then.

She wished she could tell her mother that she was healing, that she actually went out with a man without fear—or too much anyway. She was making progress.

In the middle of her letter her doorbell rang. It must be Kathryn wanting to talk, Senetra thought as she pushed herself out of the chair and padded to the door.

Through the peephole she saw—Alex. It couldn't be. She opened the door. Kathryn and Rick stood behind Alex.

"My gosh. What are you do—" Her words were smothered by his kiss.

"How did you manage to get away?"

"I've got one day. I have to leave tomorrow afternoon," he said as everyone piled in.

Senetra frowned. Why were Rick and Kathryn there?

"He came to the bar thinking you were there," Rick said, coming into the room and closing the door behind him.

"I see."

"We were arguing," Kathryn said, frustration evident in her speech. "About the same issue you and I discussed earlier."

"Spring break," Senetra mumbled, not quite grasping why they were bringing it up now. Why didn't they go back to Kathryn's apartment and argue?

"Come in and have a seat," Senetra said.

"It's so good to see you," Alex said, kissing her lightly on the lips before he shrugged out of his coat. Senetra relaxed somewhat.

"Can I get you something to drink?" Senetra asked, wanting to ease the tension between Kathryn and Rick.

"Maybe some bourbon," Rick muttered. "Kathryn's going to keep me up all night arguing anyway."

"Sorry. Don't have any. But I can fix hot chocolate or coffee, or tea."

"Hot chocolate sounds good," Alex said, making the decision. He wanted to be alone with Senetra and he was going to get rid of those two. "So what did you want to discuss?" The others finally shed their coats.

When he passed the side table, he noticed a letter addressed to him. The envelope was off-white. Alex smiled. She actually wrote to him.

Everyone piled into the kitchen while Senetra prepared the hot chocolate.

"We were hoping you two would plan a spring vacation with us," Rick said. "Then Alex and I could do some exploring while you women did your thing."

"I won't be here," Alex said. "I've been summoned home. Of course you could always join me there. Plenty of room."

"That's an idea. Wisconsin—"

"Is not the beach," Kathryn said. "If you said Florida or the Bahamas, I'd go with you. I'm serious, Rick. We always do what you want. I want a say for a change."

"There are resorts in Wisconsin with indoor swimming pools," Alex said.

Senetra set cups of hot chocolate before them.

Kathryn wouldn't be budged. "I'm so angry with you, Rick."

Rick looked confused. "What did I do? I want to spend the time with you."

"You want to explore." She sighed. "But if Senetra agrees to go, then I'll go, too."

"I'm sorry. I'm spending the break here. I'm so far behind in work."

"You're the most organized teacher I know. You can take a week," Kathryn said.

"I can't go. It's the three of you. Alex will spend time with his family and you two can…explore or do whatever."

Kathryn started doing the hula around the room, swinging her hips, her hands in the air as she danced Hawaiian style. "Lei, anyone?" she asked.

Rick moaned. "I'm losing this fight, guys. You're no help at all."

"Sorry, buddy." Alex tried to get Rick's attention. He had all week with Kathryn. Alex didn't want to spend his one day off entertaining them.

"Drink up," Alex coaxed.

"Let's go, Rick," Kathryn said, setting her cup down.

"I haven't finished my chocolate."

"Just take the cup with you," she said, coaxing Rick up and out of the room. The door shut.

"I thought they'd never leave," Alex said, embracing Senetra.

"Alex, I miss you so much."

"I know you did, Regina. And I truly believe in our relationship. The main requirements in a long-distance relationship are trust and open communication. I trust you to tell me if there's a problem with us because I certainly want to keep you happy," he said, pulling her to him. "Can I say a proper hello?"

"Hello," she whispered, smiling. He wasn't Timothy. She had to keep reminding herself. This was Alex, a totally different man.

Senetra was deeply touched and when they kissed, more of her heart opened to him. She couldn't believe he was here, that he'd spent the money he could put into his savings for a plane ride to visit her on his one day off.

She tightened her arms around him, holding him close.

The kiss was urgent and exploratory.

"I'm glad I came," he said.

"Yeah, me, too."

"I'd love to take you home spring break to meet my family," Alex said.

She glanced down. "I can't go. For the reason I gave before."

Alex wondered how long it would take her to trust him or if she ever would. But from the kiss he could feel a change and that was good. And she hadn't said no yet to the summer trip. It would be in Alaska where she felt safe.

He linked an arm around her waist and they walked to the sofa together. "So, what were you doing before I arrived?"

"Believe it or not, writing letters."

"Oh?"

"One to you and one for my mother."

His eyebrows quirked. "I noticed my name on one of them."

"You want to open it now?"

They sat on the couch and she reached across him to retrieve it and handed it to him.

He slid his finger beneath the flap, opened the card and read it.

"I thought your father might want the picture," Senetra said when he didn't speak. "Or I could have another one made for him."

"He'll love it," he said softly, "but I'd rather have one of you."

Senetra glanced away. "I take pictures. I'm not in them."

"Well," he said, sliding his hands up her arms. "Let's enjoy tonight."

Was he letting it go that easily? She tensed, waiting for the demand for an explanation. But when he said nothing more, she let her pent-up breath go and relaxed against him. "I'm all for that."

Later on, the fire was dying out in the bedroom, and Alex went to the balcony to get more wood. It was cold outside, and after coaxing the fire back to life, he climbed under the covers and pulled Senetra close to him.

"Ohhh. You're cold."

"It'll be toasty soon," he said, kissing her neck. "You're warm and comfortable—and sweet." He ran his hands up her thighs and teased them apart, stroking her inner thigh.

"That feels good."

Dorothelia walked beside George through the impressive stable and sighed. Some of the Thoroughbred horses leaned their heads over the gate, and George patted them or fed them carrots. Dorothelia held the bucket with the carrots.

"What is it?" he asked.

"For the last few years I was constantly worried about Senetra. Even when she'd disappeared. I knew Timothy was searching for her and I never knew when he'd find her. So I lived in this constant state of fear. I know you understand because you're a father."

George grasped her hand and held her gently and Dorothelia felt comforted.

"I was worrying again and suddenly I remembered that I don't have to worry any longer. She's safe. How long is it going to take for me to remember that? How long before the fear leaves my heart?"

George smiled. "I don't know. But it doesn't happen overnight. She'll stay safe. I wish she'd felt comfortable enough to come to me."

"It was a rushed arrangement. She made plans on her own. She didn't want me involved." Dorothelia stopped by a stall. "My husband died a month before she was born and I was devastated. And then I had her. It was like I had a piece of him, you know. I know Mackenzie was her biological father, but my husband loved her from the time I got pregnant, was more excited than I was. He wrote her books, tales of wisdom. Taped little messages even. Having her made the pain less," Dorothelia said. "I loved my husband. Really loved him. We were married fifteen years. And when she came, the love I had was like a pain in my gut. She was everything to me. Has always been. We were so close, George." She looked at him beseechingly. "She was always so good. She wasn't perfect, but I think she always thought she had to live up to a certain standard, maybe because of her father. But it just tore me apart when I found out Timothy was abusing her. And when he beat her the last time. Oh, George…"

She dropped the bucket of carrots and covered her face with her hands. George gathered her tightly in his arms as the tears rolled from her eyes. He found his own eyes wet and he wasn't a man who cried easily. But now…

"I wanted to hurt him the way he hurt my daughter. I've never wanted a man dead before."

"I understand."

"She didn't grow up with a father. She doesn't know what true love can be between a man and woman. I just hope her experience with him hasn't killed the possibility of love. You know what I mean?" Wiping the tears away, she gazed at him.

"I know exactly what you mean. But you're forgetting she's her mother's child, too. And in you I see strength. Your daughter must possess that strength, too. I don't think he was capable of taking that away from her. She had the strength to leave him, not once, but three times. She was determined to have her freedom regardless of what he threatened." He tilted her chin with his forefinger. "She will heal and she'll live a productive life."

"Oh, George, you are a wonderful, caring man." She brushed his chest lightly and George felt the touch to his heart. "I wish she could have known you. I wish my husband could have known you. Your son gave us such a priceless, wonderful and precious gift in my daughter."

George thought of Noelle, Jasmine and now Senetra. "I know exactly how you feel."

Dorothelia's face was mere inches from his own. Tears glistened in her lashes. She could not have looked more beautiful. Her hand was still on his chest. George lowered his head and kissed her. And when she didn't pull away, he enclosed her in the circle of his arms, her soft body pressed against his.

"Oh, Dorothelia," he whispered against her lips. She'd turned red with desire. He swallowed hard. "I hope I haven't overstepped myself. But...you must know I find you a very attractive and endearing woman."

"Oh. It's been..."

"Come to the Kentucky Derby with me. I have a horse racing at the Churchill Downs."

"I—"

"Say yes." He brushed her hair from her face. "Say yes," he repeated.

"Yes," she whispered, and he kissed her again with the sounds of Thoroughbreds around them.

Chapter 9

Later that week at work, Alex was leaving the gym and couldn't wait another minute to talk to Senetra. "What was your day like?" he asked.

"The seniors are chomping at the bit for spring break and graduation. It's almost the end of the year and they're more interested in freedom than homework and papers."

"It must be a real chore for your students and for you," he said.

"For them it is. But I can remember the excitement of my senior year, so I understand and try not to be an ogre."

"Ogre? You could never be that. You're too sweet."

"Some of my students wouldn't agree with you."

"So, do most of your students travel to warmer climates during spring break?"

"I really don't know."

"I'm going to stop by for a couple of days before I visit my family if it's okay with you." His father had called him a couple times a week to make sure he hadn't changed his mind.

"I'd love to see you."

"It'll be good to see my father and nieces and nephews."

"I bet you're a favorite uncle."

"Yeah. I enjoyed them last summer."

"I don't have any siblings. Must be nice to have five of them. All the noise and companionship. Family gatherings must be great."

"Yeah." They shared a quiet moment of contemplation. "Wish you would change your mind about going with me?"

"I can't," she said softly, and Alex wished she trusted him as much as he trusted her. But then he had less to lose.

The relationship was still pretty new. "What about the end of the year? Will you consider going on the southwest tour with me? Should I put in for leave?"

"Yes," she said softly, and the sweet sound zipped through Alex like a hot flame. Surprise kept him silent for a beat.

"Shall I book one room or two?" He held his breath, hoping she'd say one.

"I'll take care of my room."

"No, you won't. This is my treat."

"I'll be more comfortable if I pay for my own, Alex."

Alex heard the underlying steel in her voice, but her paying her own way didn't sit well with him. "Regina, I invited you. I'm okay with the two rooms, but I'll—"

"Either I pay for my room or I won't go." Her tone was stubborn.

"Okay. I'll book the rooms. You'll pay for yours." If he pushed her any harder she'd pull out altogether and Alex didn't want that. He had to remember small steps. Although he'd spent Saturday night in her apartment, maybe an entire week sharing a room was too much for her at this point.

"So, have you had dinner?"

"Actually, I ate a bowl of clam chowder and bread from the bakery." She'd made another pot of clam chowder with the clams she'd frozen.

"I shared some of your chowder and had to hide the rest. They're still asking when I'm coming back to get more."

"Next time you're here we'll go clamming again," Senetra said, and Alex breathed a sigh of relief. She wasn't marking him off her calendar. He hadn't blown it.

"It should be warmer."

"Only a little."

Alex didn't want to talk about the weather or clamming. He wanted to make love to her over the phone, but kept it low-key. The situation was too delicate for him to unwind that way.

Senetra had mixed feelings. She knew she was sending conflicting messages. She made love with Alex, but she needed to be in control at the same time. She had depended too much on Timothy. No, Timothy had forced her to become dependent on him. She didn't want to depend on anyone now but herself. She wanted to pay her own way.

Alex must think she was crazy. Making issues over small matters, but they were important to her and her feelings mattered. She valued her independence and that she could provide for herself.

"So, what are you wearing? I need a verbal picture since I don't have a physical one."

She wore sweatpants and a T-shirt. "Oh, an ice-blue thong that came in the mail with this demi-cup bra. In the same color."

Silence.

"Alex, are you there?"

A swift breath. "Woman, just the thought of that…"

"I have a surprise for you when you return."

"I can't wait," he said.

After they hung up, Senetra moved to her computer. She hadn't thought of buying anything sexy in a very long time. Wouldn't it be nice to buy some sexy under-wear and a nightgown? Her mother had tucked new bottles of makeup in her bag, but Senetra hadn't bothered to open them. After ordering catalogues from a few Web sites, she also ordered lingerie and undergarments and felt feminine and powerful. She paid extra to have them delivered quickly. Alex would appreciate the effort. He wouldn't use her femininity against her.

The next week, Senetra got a letter from her contact in Washington State.

A private investigator came by the school where you taught. The principal wrote to me, giving me a heads-up that someone was searching for you. Never fear, he didn't give anything away. And he waited a week to mail the letter, putting it in a PO box when he was traveling. There's no connection between us except that we met at a convention years ago, so don't worry that your location has been compromised.

Oh, my God. Won't I ever have peace?
She continued to read that her mother was spending a lot of time traveling recently. She'd been gone for almost a month. Good for her, Senetra thought. In the past she was too concerned to leave for very long because of her situation with Timothy. Now she could have some fun for a change. Senctra wondered if Rachel went with her.

But the fact that someone was looking for her concerned her. She couldn't even think of going away with Alex. What if…? No. She wouldn't do this to herself. It was perfectly safe to travel in locations Timothy's investigator was sure not to search. Timothy would never find her here. She had to get on with her life.

If Timothy's goons did happen to find her, they'd

stand out and she would easily slip away before they reached her.

If only Charles was a better karate teacher. She sent an e-mail to the community center's director requesting a new karate teacher.

The week passed with lightning-quick speed. Senetra was waiting at the Spit when Alex got off the plane. She'd told him not to rent a car. They could use hers. As soon as his tall form touched the ground, he opened his arms wide and she ran into them.

"Oh, my gosh. It seems like forever," she said as their lips parted.

"My God. You look even better in person." He regarded her seriously. "Two weeks is too long—way too long."

"It is."

"Let's go. I'm going to drop my gear at Rick's place, then…whatever."

"Okay."

But he dragged her into his arms again for another long kiss before they started on their journey.

Twenty minutes later, they shoved open the door to Senetra's apartment. From the plane to her apartment, desire built to humongous proportions.

The desire sizzling between them was burning even hotter.

Alex shrugged out of his coat, trying not to jump her bones the minute he got in her door. He wanted more than sex. She'd come to mean a lot to him in the short time they'd been together, but he dragged her into his arms again and before he knew it, they were hopping out of their clothes until the only clothing left on her were her bra and thong. Alex stopped, gazed at the amazing sight of her encased in two tiny scraps of fabric. She wore a thong. An ice-blue thong, exactly like the one she had described over the phone.

"My gosh, what a change," he said, holding her back so he could get his fill. Her body looked amazing. Her skin blushed. "And all for me?" He noticed the light dusting of makeup that brightened her already glowing skin.

"Woman, you take my breath away," he finally said when, tried of waiting, she reached for him.

"I don't know about you," she said, closing the distance between them, "but it's been a long time."

"Too long," he said, dragging her close to him and brushing his lips across her face, and with his hands on her backside dragged her solidly against him. But she wouldn't let him take it slow. She rubbed her body against him, driving his need out of control.

"I'm trying to keep it slow, baby."

"I don't want it slow. I want it hot and furious."

"Woman." With her magical fingers, she stroked him until he could stand it no longer. And he caressed her body from her face to her feet, listening to her moans of pleasure. He stroked her until she begged for release. Only then did he drag the thong from her and open her legs wide. He caressed and kissed her intimately, until she cried out in fulfillment, which was music to his ears.

He gazed down on her. There was nothing more

gratifying than a woman in the afterglow of an orgasm. He brushed her hair gently from her face and she looked up at him in wonder and amazement. The fact that he put that glow on her face did fantastic things to his body.

He was hard and more than ready for her, but he gave her a moment to enjoy her pleasure. Then she reached for him and her breath hitched in his throat as he flipped her on top of him, letting her glide the condom on him and positioning herself. She eased down on him until he filled her completely. For a moment, he didn't move. He wanted to enjoy this moment of sweet contact.

Her hair was wild. A nipple peeked over the top edge of her bra cup. He released the front clasp, but left the straps dangling on her shoulders. Her full breasts spilled into his hands as he stroked them.

Then he grasped her hips and they began to move. He leaned up to brush his lips over her breasts, to suck gently on her nipple.

Her movements increased and he deepened his thrusts; they abandoned themselves to the pleasure of the moment.

He stroked her clitoris and her breath hitched in her throat, her cries and moans urging him on.

Their thrusts varied from deep and penetrating to more shallow, increasing their sexual pleasure with their teasing playful actions.

She glided her hands up his chest, then followed with sweet kisses.

He could tell she was close to coming when her thighs tightened against him.

Alex was at the end of his rope, too. He could stand it no longer. He grasped her hips again, and increased the intensity. They moved in rhythm until they both exploded into a new kaleidoscope of pleasure and completion.

Senetra fell on his chest.

Alex stroked her back. She'd drained every bit of energy from him.

Later that night, with Alex sleeping peacefully beside her, Senetra couldn't sleep. His breathing was even and deep and his arm rested across her waist. Senetra ran her hands softly over his hand, her thoughts troubling her.

How could they go forward when she couldn't tell Alex about her past? It wasn't fair. She felt guilty because he was so forthcoming with her. He was good to her.

Stop beating yourself up. The object was first to stay alive. Everything else was secondary. Maybe one day she could tell him. She wished she could share her worries that someone was still looking for her, but she had to keep that close to her chest.

Alex arrived in Wisconsin earlier than he'd told his dad to expect him. He rented a car at the airport and drove directly to his father's rural home. It was two stories and lights shone from all the windows.

His dad came out on the porch frowning, wondering who the stranger was. When Alex climbed out of the car, the older man's face split into a huge grin as he lumbered down from the porch into the yard without the aid of a cane.

"Aren't you a sight for sore eyes?" the older man said, grabbing him in a hug and patting Alex's back.

"It's good to see you, too, Dad. And you're walking like a new man."

His dad chuckled. "Feel like one, too. Thought I'd never be walking again." He danced a little step. "Much less getting around like this. Thanks, son. I couldn't have done it without you." He shouldered Alex again.

"No need to thank me. It was you cursing through therapy. There was no doubt that you'd walk," Alex said, leaning back to arm's length to gaze at the older man. "You're looking good."

Alex retrieved his bag from the trunk and they walked side by side to the house. His brothers, sisters and their children were already there. His father had called, telling them the night before.

He hadn't been home for more than a day or so in two years. He'd spent the time he'd usually get off working, making extra money. After the huge fight between his siblings and with the breakup with Jessica, there wasn't a need for frequent visits. He talked to his dad often and followed his progress closely.

Actually, his sisters-in-law called and e-mailed him, updating him often, especially on his nieces and nephews.

Most of the family was in the living room, watching the news.

"Look who's home," his father said, smiling.

"Well, the prodigal son returns at last," one of his brothers said.

"Welcome home," his older brother said, standing. "It's good to see you, man." He came over and gave him a one-shoulder hug.

"It's good to be back."

"Uncle Alex!" one of his nephews called out before he barreled into him.

"Hey, you've grown ten feet, sport."

"Naw."

They exchanged mock punches, before Alex hugged him. The boy was thirteen, but his voice was beginning to change.

"You're almost a man. I've got to keep tabs on you. Got a girlfriend?"

His nephew laughed. His other nieces and nephews greeted him and one of them carried his bag to his old room.

It was a couple of hours before he could escape. It still wasn't too late to call Senetra.

They talked an hour on the phone.

He thought his dad was in bed, but when Alex went to the kitchen for a drink of water, his father was sitting at the table.

"Can't sleep?" Alex leaned against the counter.

"Just happy all my family is home, that's all. Don't want to miss a minute of it."

Alex smiled.

"You were on the phone for a while."

Alex took a swallow of water. "I met this lady in Alaska. She's great."

"You like her a lot?"

"Yeah."

"I'm glad," his father said. "Are you going to see Jessica while you're here?"

"If our paths cross," he said. "I'm not going to search her out."

"Hard not to as she attends the same church."

"Yeah. Regina sent you something."

"Is that your new friend's name?" his father asked. Alex nodded.

"What did she send me?"

"Back in a sec." Alex retrieved the framed photo from his room and gave it to his father.

"Hey. This is from the tournament you told me about?"

Alex nodded. A couple of his brothers came into the room and looked at the picture.

"You've become quite the fisherman," his older brother, Samuel, said.

"Still amateur, but it's fun."

His dad went to bed.

"Most of us are leaving in a few days," one of his brothers said. "Wish you came earlier."

Alex shrugged.

He knew his brothers wanted to talk about his decision, but their wives came in and the discussion was shelved for another time.

Alex attended church with the rest of his family. As his father was a deacon, he said a few words before the church about his joy at having all his children home, especially Alex, who was working for an oil company in Alaska. Alex could have done without the attention.

The pastor asked Alex to say a few words and Alex expressed how much he'd enjoyed the service and seeing so many familiar faces.

After the service, he couldn't get out of the door before he was waylaid again and again and commended for what he'd done for his father. And then Jessica and her husband approached. They'd all attended the same schools.

"Welcome home, man," Jessica's husband, Josh, said. "Good to see you."

"Good to see you," Alex responded with a smile, and shook Josh's hand before he kissed Jessica lightly on the cheek. She wasn't showing yet.

"Congratulations are in order. I'm really happy for you." And surprisingly, Alex meant it. He'd expected to feel regret, jealousy, loss. But he felt none of those things. He could see they were happy together although Josh seemed a little possessive. "When is the baby due?"

"October," Jessica responded.

The pastor called to Josh and he left them.

Jessica seemed nervous. "Are you really all right?"

Alex nodded.

"I just… I hate that you're out there all alone in a place where you can't date."

"I can date," Alex said. "And I do. It's a long-distance relationship, but it works."

"What does she do there?" Jessica asked.

"She's a high school teacher."

"And she's black?"

Alex nodded and chuckled. "One of only a handful in town."

"So, what happens when you leave?" Jessica asked. "Will she come back here with you?"

"We'll figure that out when it happens. Right now I fly out to visit her every chance I get."

"I'm glad things are working out well with you. You're looking good."

"I'm glad you're happy, Jessica."

His brother Samuel signaled him. "It was nice seeing you again. Have a happy Easter," Alex said, and joined his brother.

Alex spoke to a few more parishioners on his way to the car.

"That must have been tough," Sam said.

"It wasn't."

"So you're over her?"

"Completely." And it was true. Alex couldn't wait to get back to Senetra.

It was late Sunday night, after Alex's father and the younger kids had gone to bed and the older ones were either outside horsing around or watching TV, that the brothers and sisters closed the door to the kitchen and sat at the country kitchen table to talk. Alex geared up for the confrontation as his older brother took the lead.

"It's not that we don't appreciate what you did, Alex,

and we're not ganging up on you. It's just that it should have been a family decision," one of his brothers said.

"What we really want to say is thank you," Samuel said. "Dad told us selling the land was his decision. He wouldn't let you stop him. Working in Alaska was a selfless thing you did for Dad and we appreciate it."

"But—" his other brother started, the contentious one.

"We would have sat around this table arguing for hours, maybe even days with Daddy in the hospital not knowing how this was going to turn out," his older sister said.

"I'm just sorry you lost Jessica," his younger sister said.

"It wasn't meant to be."

"But you loved each other."

"I thought I did, but I found someone better for me."

"We haven't seen you for two years. Just don't let that happen again. Because we missed you," his older sister said.

"Alaska isn't that far away that you can't make it back for Christmas or Thanksgiving," his younger sister said.

"I hear you loud and clear," Alex retorted. "I missed you, too."

"You all know damn well you would have argued to kingdom come. Since when have we agreed on anything? We could have visited him," the brother next to him muttered.

"Just like always, Johnny-come-lately. We'd already solved this thing."

"I'm just stating the truth whether you want to hear it or not."

"Just tell me you didn't sacrifice a lifetime of happiness when you lost Jessica," his older sister said.

"It's exactly what I'm telling you," he said.

"So, will we get to meet this new woman?"

"Who said there was a new one?" Alex said. "Like I tell you all my business."

Everyone glared at him until he relented.

"You might have to come to Alaska to meet her. She won't come here."

"Why not?"

Alex shrugged. "She has her reasons."

"Now, you didn't fall for some weirdo, did you?" his older sister asked.

One of his brothers punched him in the side. "We've got a family of weirdos. Don't have to go all the way to Alaska for that."

"But your home is still here," Samuel said.

Alex was ready to put down roots. Homer was a nice community. He didn't think for a moment Senetra would come back here.

"We'll see," Alex said but wouldn't commit.

"My wife's been bugging me about an Alaskan cruise for years," Samuel said finally. "Flying there will be even better."

Chapter 10

After Alex went to his room, he called Senetra. It was twelve in Wisconsin, but only nine in Homer.

"How did your trip go?" she asked, but sounded a little subdued.

"Better than I thought. I'm leaving early tomorrow morning." He lowered his voice. "I'm looking forward to seeing you."

"Me, too."

"You want to see you?" Alex joked, but wondered what was going on.

"You, silly."

Pressure left Alex's chest.

"How long can you stay?"

"I'm leaving Thursday morning. I'll be with you until Sunday."

"I'll see if I can plan something for the weekend," she said.

After they hung up, Alex considered asking his cousin what was going on with Timothy, but decided not to. Eventually, when Senetra began to trust him, he was hoping she'd tell her story. Until then, he wouldn't mention Timothy.

"How was your trip home?" she asked when Alex arrived Friday afternoon.

"It was great. Made up with the siblings. Had a great time with the nieces and nephews. A couple of my brothers are coming here to meet you this summer."

Apprehension invaded her good mood. Meeting his family meant pictures and she couldn't let anyone take pictures of her. His family would think it strange if she refused to take them, but it was a small world and she'd been careful so far.

"Are you sure that's a good idea?" Senetra hedged. "It's not cheap coming here. We've only been dating a little while."

"I want my family to meet you and I know you won't go to Wisconsin. Or will you?"

Senetra bit down on her lip as her gaze skimmed him. "I'm not ready to meet them."

A moment of silence preceded his "Then they'll meet me in Anchorage. They don't know where you are, only that I've met you."

Senetra felt a little better, but not much. Still, she

wasn't going to let her doubts spoil their time together. Their relationship might not even last the summer.

Senetra had suggested they take a walk.

"You're quiet," Alex said. The park was quiet, also.

"I'm gathering my thoughts."

"I sensed something was wrong the last time I spoke with you. What is it?"

"Alex, I care a lot about you, but I shouldn't have started a relationship with you."

Startled, Alex stopped and stared at her. "Where did this come from?"

"I can't give you details so don't ask me. But someone is searching for me. If he finds me, he'll kill me, and if you're here, he could very well kill you, too." She stared at him with anguish. "I can't take the chance of that happening."

"I thought we had a relationship. That means both of us discuss things and make decisions based on facts." Alex was beginning to see the problem his brothers and sisters had with him two years ago. He'd thought he was in the right the last couple of years; he hadn't seen the situation from their point of view. "I couldn't live with something happening to you because of me. So let's discuss it," Alex said.

Senetra shook her head. "It's not like that. If you aren't involved with me, my ex wouldn't come after you."

"Do you really expect me to give up our relationship because he might come after you?"

"There's no might about it. I'm hiding because of him."

"Obviously you chose this location for a reason. So that means more than likely *he* won't come here."

"That doesn't mean I can't be found. He's found me before."

"How long have you been here?"

"Several months."

"So obviously you've done a damn good job of hiding out."

Frustrated, Senetra said, "Don't you understand? I can never go home. You can't have a picture of me on your bedside table. I can't visit your family. There's so much involved here. And I should have told you all this in the beginning."

"I'm in Alaska, too, and if we take this relationship further, then I can continue to work where I am, or I can teach here."

"That's no way to live. I hate having to live this way, hate that I can't even call my mother. If she's sick, I won't know. If she needs me, I'm not there. It was just the two of us. And—"

"Senetra..." He pulled her to him. "Baby, don't distress yourself this way."

But Senetra pushed away. "If you wanted to travel, I couldn't go with you. I'd have to spend my life right here."

"That's not your fault."

"That doesn't matter. It's a fact of my life. The price I have to pay for marrying the wrong man. But it shouldn't be yours."

Alex pulled her to him again and rubbed his hand over her back. "You're stressing out over nothing. I'm not making light of your feelings, but this feels right to me. This relationship. You and me. I… You're special, and I'm not letting that go because of your fear. Because your ex might show up. I don't frighten easily."

Senetra pushed back. "He almost killed me. It's not about being brave. Domestic violence can happen to both men and women."

"Nobody should have to put up with that crap."

She looked at him, trying to get him to understand. "It's… I don't know what I'd do if anything happened to you."

"Calm down, Regina. We'll cross that bridge when we get to it. These people, this community protects you. He's not going to be able to waltz in here and have his way with you. Don't destroy what we have because of something that might happen. You just can't live that way. Because it could just as easily not happen."

"It's the only way I can live," she said. "As long as the laws don't really protect people who are abused, I have to live in a prison my ex made for me."

"Then we'll live in it together. Sharing your life has to be better than going it alone. Don't give up on us."

Senetra blew out a long breath. "You make it so hard."

"I want to make it impossible."

"I can't promise you more than what we already have. You know that."

"I'm not asking for more."

She moaned, her face pressed against his chest. He rubbed her back.

He wanted to take her inside her apartment and make

love to her until her fears faded away. But he couldn't have her thinking that all he wanted was sex. And their discussion was too serious to take lightly.

He couldn't believe it, but he was actually falling in love with her. And he couldn't tell her. It was the last thing she'd want to hear right now.

He tilted her chin, bent and pressed his lips to hers.

"I've been alone for two years. Since we've been together, I don't feel so alone anymore," he said quietly. "People need people. You can live your life without me and I can live mine without you, but the joy I feel with you wouldn't be there. It's the special moments that we share that make it all worthwhile," he said. "We'll find a way to make things work, Regina. Even if my family has to come here to see you."

Senetra's lips trembled as she held back tears when Alex kissed her again. "Oh, Alex, why couldn't I have met you before my ex came into my life? Why couldn't I see beneath his charming exterior?"

"You saw what he wanted you to see. And maybe we wouldn't have appreciated each other this much if we'd met at any other time. Things happen for a reason. If my father hadn't taken ill, I wouldn't have been here and I wouldn't have met you. If your ex hadn't been abusive, you wouldn't be here right now. We met up at the right time and at the right place for all the right reasons. It's fate," he said. "I believe that."

"Alex—"

"We'll take this one day, one week at a time. And we'll make it work. And we won't waste our time with what-ifs. Because we can't predict the future. No sense in trying."

Alex wanted to tell Senetra that he knew about her, and he knew her ex, but she wasn't ready to hear that. Maybe later on she'd trust him enough that he could tell her.

"So what are we doing tonight?"

"My friend is exhibiting her paintings in the gallery. I promised her I'd go."

"Good thing I brought my suit with me."

Actually, four artists exhibited at the show. People from miles away attended.

Two amateurs exhibited, but the stars were one world-renowned painter and a very popular Inuit carver.

Rarely did Senetra get an opportunity to pull out formal wear, but tonight she wore the plain, long, black dress that had hung in her closet for months.

Alex whistled when he saw her. The pearls her mother had given her for college graduation lay cool against her neck. They were a perfect complement to the dress.

Alex looked great in his black suit. She smoothed the perfectly placed lapels as an excuse to touch him.

"You're handsome." She stood on tiptoes to kiss him. His warm, strong arms came around her.

"You look fantastic," he said, and the light in his eyes assured her he meant every word. "If we don't leave, we won't leave," he said, nuzzling her neck.

They went out into the chilled night.

At the gallery, waiters carried around small trays of assorted hors d'oeuvres and champagne flutes filled nearly to the brim. Senetra took one that was only half-filled. She felt comfortable enough to drink a little. Alex knew her past. She wasn't going to drink enough to lose control.

They walked around to view and discuss the various pieces.

Senetra introduced Alex to her friend and they discussed her work before the curator whisked her away to introduce her to a prospective buyer.

"Do you see anything you like?" Alex asked.

"I like a lot of them."

He steered her to an obscure wall to view a well-lit painting by one of the up-and-coming artists. "This would fit over your fireplace."

How could a painting display opposing emotions? It was peaceful, yet energetic in some ways. Senetra studied the painting closely. It was a seascape, but not one that you'd see reproduced a million times. It was a unique creation of Kachemak Bay, but not with boats in the background, rather a bear and a dolphin frolicking. The water seemed peaceful in some places and roiling in others. She could have looked at it all evening.

"I love it," Senetra said.

"Then I'll get it for you."

He was saving for his future and Senetra wanted to decline, but by the look on his face, giving the gift to her pleased him.

"Thank you. I'll treasure it." She watched as the

curator put a Sold sign on the painting. She'd have it hung as soon as the show was over.

They made fantastic love after the show, and afterward Senetra lay halfway across Alex and brushed her hand across chest. She liked touching him.

"My mother would like you."

"Think so?" He felt warm and strong.

"Yeah. She never liked my ex. Thought he was too slick," Senetra said. "She was right."

"Is she one of those 'I told you so' mothers?"

"Never. She was always supportive. We were best friends." Senetra told him about her father and how she met him through his books and tapes.

This was good, too. She rubbed her foot down his leg. The light from the fireplace flickered across Senetra's face. Alex memorized the nuances of her face. The way her eyes lit up when she smiled. The tiny dimple was easy to miss if he wasn't looking closely. The perfect curve of her lips. And most of all, her expressions. The expressions on her face were like scenes in a book. From the guarded look when he'd first arrived, to the pleased, completely satisfied and half-erotic expression right now. If he couldn't have a photo, he'd have the memories.

But most of all, he treasured the insight into her past. It meant she was beginning to trust him.

Kathryn returned Sunday night, exclaiming about her trip. Senetra sat on Kathryn's bed while she unpacked and they talked.

"Oh, my gosh. We should have done this ages ago. The sun was warm. We took a helicopter tour over the volcano. Of course Rick would have rather walked it, but this was my vacation and I was calling the shots."

Senetra laughed.

"And I'm exhausted. We toured most of the day. Every day. Rick doesn't know how to relax. We toured aquariums, we went snorkeling, to pineapple fields and coffee and cocoa factories. You name it, we did it."

"Sounds like fun."

"You have to go. Alex is more low-key, so you'll have more walks on the beach. I only got one day to lie out in the sun."

"Trust me, I won't be lying in the sun."

"Why not? It's fun."

"I'll take your word for it."

"So, did Alex visit?" Kathryn asked.

"Twice. On his way to Wisconsin and on his way back. He left an hour before you arrived."

"So it's working out. I did a good deed after all, although it was Rick's idea to set you two up."

"It's working out so far."

Chapter 11

When Dorothelia arrived at the Louisville Airport, a limousine picked her up and whisked her to the hotel. The place was brimming with excitement and money.

George had left her room key at the desk and she didn't have to go through the check-in procedure. A cheese and fruit tray was waiting for her in the room.

It was warm in Kentucky, and Dorothelia was itching for a shower. She sampled some of the food before she took a lengthy shower, dressed casually and waited for a call from George. He'd mentioned some function they would attend that evening. She was just about to fix herself a more substantial plate when she heard a knock at her door.

It was George and he looked quite handsome in casual slacks and shirt.

She gathered a breath and opened the door for him.

"My dear. I am so happy to see you."

"Oh, George." Dorothelia's face felt hot as George advanced into the room. He closed the door firmly behind him before he gently encircled her in his arms. She tingled all over at the feel of those strong hands on her. The kiss was sweet and needy, desperate as they were to be with each other after parting for so long. They'd talked every day since she left. Dorothelia hadn't expected to feel this way about a man at this time in her life.

"I missed you," he said as their lips parted. "And you kissed me as if you missed me, too."

"I did." Dorothelia had needed to go home to take care of some business. She rushed through everything, including visiting a milliner to get a special hat made for the Derby. She felt like a silly teenager. There was something fresh and energizing about new love. *Get real, Dorothelia. Deep affection is a better term.*

"Is the room comfortable?" George asked, but he was regarding her, not the room.

"Very. Thank you. Would you like something to snack on? I have a beautiful fruit and cheese tray."

"And perhaps a glass of wine to go with it," George said, glancing around for the first time, pleased that everything was as he'd requested.

"Of course."

George had great plans for their stay in Kentucky.

The only stain on their happiness was the private investigator's inability to find Senetra. George had to give it to Senetra. She was an intelligent young lady. He was growing frustrated. He couldn't wait to meet her and he knew it would please Dorothelia when he did. He had plans and he doubted she'd fall in line until Senetra was found.

Dorothelia prepared two plates and handed one to him. "I'm surprised he hasn't been able to find her yet. With technology being what it is, it shouldn't be that difficult."

"She's done a terrific job of hiding this time. The investigator said she didn't make the silly errors most people make. It's going to take a while, but he'll eventually find her. I have no doubt of that."

"It can't be soon enough."

"She's safe. That's what's important."

Dorothelia's gaze touched his. "You're right. I'm being selfish. Her safety is what's important. And this is your time. I won't bring up depressing news."

He gathered her hand in his. "Don't hide from me, Dorothelia. If you're concerned, I want to know."

Dorothelia smiled. "You're a wonderful man, George Avery.

"With that. Let's eat our snack and enjoy our time here."

Dorothelia appeared too edgy to sit down. She stood as the horses flew around the track. Her heart thumped in her chest. The jockey held Thunder back in the beginning, but during the final stretch, he passed one horse, then another as if he'd gotten a second wind.

"Go, go, go…" she entreated. The finish line was coming much too quickly. "Just a little faster. Run, run, run.…" She clutched George's hand.

Dorothelia fascinated George. He was seeing everything from her fresh eyes. Her excitement was contagious. Finally, the jockey was pressing the horse to run full-out, and George's heart caught in his throat, too.

Could this finally happen?

For the first time in decades, would a River Oak Thoroughbred win the Kentucky Derby? If Thunder won this one—just this one—he wouldn't have to race another race. He would serve as a Thoroughbred stud.

He clutched Dorothelia's hand, trying to keep his emotions under control. Colin, Noelle, Jasmine and Drake showed no such compunction. They were all standing and yelling, just as most of the crowd was. It might seem like a dignified crowd, but this race could mean big money. And big money brought them all to their feet.

Silently he urged Thunder to win, too. They were almost neck to neck, mere yards from the finish line. His heart skipped. Thunder inched forward, finishing a mere head in front of the second horse.

George went weak in the knees. He held on to the railing to keep from falling. He could leave his grandchildren—all three of them—a grand legacy. Stud fees would skyrocket.

"What a grand finish," Dorothelia said, her eyes bright with excitement and tears.

He'd won enough races that they got great stud fees for Thunder anyway, but this was the Kentucky Derby. Their fees would now double. He'd begin making deals before the day was over.

"Congratulations!" Everyone around them was shaking hands, hugging and kissing. He was filled with so much joy he could have leaped out of his skin.

"What're you waiting for?" Colin asked. "Let's go to the winner's circle."

Dorothelia clasped her hands to his cheeks and kissed him, shocking him to the soles of his shoes.

"Let's go," Colin repeated.

Dorothelia looked confused. "Where are you going?"

"To the winner's circle."

George extended his elbow for her to take. "Let's go."

"Oh, this is your time," she said, but George insisted. She was still flushed with excitement as she slipped her hand through his arm.

"Only one thing could make this more complete," George murmured as they made their way through the crowd. He took the ring box out of his breast pocket.

"This isn't how I'd planned to present this to you," he said, but he took the ring out of the box and handed it to her.

"Will you marry me?" he asked, and chuckled a little nervously. "I should have waited for a more appropriate time when we were alone and could take our own special moment and do this properly. Even go down on one knee."

"Oh, George." Now she clasped her hands on her own jaws.

"I love you, Dorothelia. You've brought joy into my life I thought was gone forever. Say you'll marry me."

"Oh, George," she repeated. "I love you. I want to marry you, I really do."

He slid the ring onto her finger. Dorothelia's eyes watered.

"This is absolutely… It's too much," she said, tears glistening on her lashes. One escaped, sliding down her face.

George paused and wiped it with his thumb. The center diamond was four carats, but it definitely wasn't too much for her. Nothing was too much for her.

"It's perfect for you, my love."

She wrapped her arms around him and he closed his eyes briefly as he hugged her back. *Thank you, God,* was all he could think.

Colin urged them to move on again.

He kissed her soft fingers as they made it to the track, where a blanket of roses was being placed on Thunder. They were indeed the winners of the Kentucky Derby and their horse and jockey were at the winner's circle.

George and Dorothelia did not get a private moment again until they were in George's suite where they sought out a quiet corner to talk. The catering staff was busily setting out hors d'ouevres as George was expecting a parade of people to come through.

"We have to find Senetra. That has to be our priority," Dorothelia was saying quietly.

"Dorothelia, dear, we will eventually find her. She wouldn't want you to put your life on hold, and I hope she isn't putting hers on hold, either. We hope she's happy wherever she is and that she can trust enough to fall in love again. I don't wish for her to be alone."

"I know, but…I'm afraid to be away from home too much. If she needs me, she won't know how to reach me. She doesn't know I'm in Virginia."

"If she can't reach you at home, she can reach your friends, right? And she knows your cell phone number."

Dorothelia nodded.

"I love you, dear. Life is too precious to waste a minute of it."

"I'll marry you, but let's wait awhile. I'd like Senetra to be part of our wedding, if possible. I just… It won't be the same without her." She glanced at George with an expression that made it impossible for him to refuse her anything. "I want her to meet you. You're such a wonderful man, George."

George wanted to argue the point further, but he acquiesced. "We'll set a date in two months. Will that work for you?"

Dorothelia nodded.

"But in the meantime, I'd like you to spend most of your time in Virginia—with me. I'm willing to wait, but not live apart," he said, and hurried on. "I don't expect to take liberties as my other grandchildren are in the house, and I'd like to set a good example. But having you near me will be enough."

"Well, George, I don't expect you to be a saint. You are a handsome man, after all."

George sucked in a breath, felt the heat shoot through his body. It was a good thing Dorothelia had a separate room. He'd wanted her to be able to relax without all the hubbub. Of course, in the back of his mind, he was thinking of other pleasures.

"In that case, I'll be visiting you in your room tonight," he said, and had the pleasure of watching Dorothelia blush prettily. "Will you give me that much?"

"Yes."

Summer at last. Her students had graduated and had turned wild. Senetra always thought there was logic behind that. The parents would be so stressed out by the end of August they'd welcome their children's departure to college.

Her freezer was overpacked with salmon, and now halibut, along with enough clams to make several batches of soup and fry.

Rick and Alex had participated in a halibut derby and caught a two-hundred-fifty-pound fish. Senetra was one person, for heaven's sake, and although she didn't mind cooking, she and Alex often ate out when he visited. In the apartment, he had a one-track mind. Her bedroom, her couch—they'd tried out the entire place with their lovemaking.

How much fish could she eat? She'd talked Alex into shipping some to his father, because he never took any back with him. He gave his share to her, part of which was stored in Rick's freezer—which never had a chance to empty anyway since he was always fishing and adding more. The good thing was they didn't let food go to waste. They shared with others, too, especially seniors who couldn't fish as they did when they were younger.

Dorothelia loved fish. If only she could ship some to her mother. But if Timothy's people found out, it would give them a new vantage point for their search.

He'd taught her a well-learned lesson. By now, what love he'd had for her must have died.

Senetra had some misgivings about her trip with Alex, but that wasn't unusual. She'd learned to feel the fear and move forward anyway.

"Hi, Ms. Novak."

Senetra waved at Mark and his friend.

"Where you off to?" Mark asked.

"I'm taking the southwest ferry tour. The write-up of it in the brochures sounded great."

"You'll love it. My dad used to take us practically every summer. We used to camp out when we didn't stay on the boat."

"I won't be camping out." No, thank you. Her nights would be spent in the comfort of a stateroom.

He chuckled. "You're missing half the fun."

"What are your plans for the summer?"

"My dad took a group of tourists out for a week," Mark said.

"Is he deep-sea fishing this summer?"

"He'll make one long trip, but the rest of the summer

he takes out small groups of rich guys. There are about five on this trip. I'll be going with him on other trips." He shrugged. "My summer job. I get to see how the other half lives."

Senetra knew it wasn't uncommon for a fisherman to make as much as twenty or thirty grand on such a tour.

"Take care," Mark said, and pulled off in his SUV.

Senetra waved and rushed through her last-minute shopping. By the time the ferry took off with both her and Alex on it, she was ready for some R & R.

There was only one thing she would change. She wished she'd gotten one room instead of insisting on two.

When Alex pulled her into his arms, she felt the sunlight was shining down on her.

Alex rented an SUV for the day they toured Unalaska and the Dutch Harbor islands that were part of the chain of Aleutian Islands. These two islands were connected by a bridge.

It was a busy area off the Iliuliuk Bay and because of the confluence of the north Pacific Ocean and the Bering Sea, it was one of the richest fisheries in the world. Dutch Harbor was known for its natural deepwater port. More than four hundred ships arrived there each year from fourteen countries. And an excess of eight hundred million pounds of seafood was processed there annually.

Senetra remembered some of the teachings of her history lessons.

It had rained overnight and the day started out foggy and cold, but once the fog burned off, it turned bright and sunny.

They observed some of the rarest arctic birds, as well as three types of whales and beautiful florae.

Near noon, it had warmed to fifty degrees and they had to shed heavy coats for thick sweatshirts.

They learned some of the history of the area. Such as in 1768 Unalaska became a trading port for the Russian fur trade industry.

They also toured the World War II museum that honored the Unangans and the American forces who'd fought the Japanese on the Attu and Kiska islands.

During that time the Unangans were forcibly removed from their homes and taken to southeast Alaska to be placed in internment camps for the next three years Many of the old and young died in the squalid and inhuman conditions.

From there, Senetra and Alex toured the beautiful and ornate Russian Orthodox Church. Senetra stopped to pray for the pure pleasure and joy of the day.

She turned to Alex. "Thank you."

He was still gazing at the church, but turned his gaze on her. "For what?"

"For bringing me on this trip." At every port she'd experienced something new and wonderful. Things she never would have experienced had she not left her town.

He smiled and placed an arm around her shoulder. "Hey, I'm enjoying it, too."

"You've been here before."

"It's different from seeing it with a couple of teenage guys glad to be away from home. But I enjoyed it with them, too. It was just different," he said. "I'm glad I'm here with you." He kissed her on the forehead. "It's time we eat. My stomach's sunk in."

Senetra patted the tightly knitted muscles. "It's not sinking in yet." But they left to find food near the dock. Senetra selected a halibut sandwich on a bun and Alex chose a lobster sandwich.

Back on the boat, they showered and rested. Touring was definitely tiring. Two hours later, Senetra came awake with Alex's kisses.

"We're going to miss dinner if we don't get up."

"Is it that late?" She was still adjusting to the midnight sun. The sun was still shining bright outside.

"We still have time to eat at a restaurant in town." He kissed her stomach and Senetra sucked in a breath. "Or we could have fun first and eat on the boat." He caressed her inner thigh, touching, then kissing just the right spot to make her moan in pleasure.

"I'm all for playing," she managed to say, because he was stroking her and she moved her hips for optimal pleasure.

She was on the brink of an orgasm and then she was falling over. Alex waited until her body had come off this high before he entered her.

He sank deep within her and stopped. She gazed at him, searching to read his thoughts.

"What is it?"

"I love you," he said.

"Alex…" Senetra was brimming over with emotions. "I love you, too." She wished she could take a snapshot, to preserve this moment forever, not the lovemaking, but the feelings, the love, the connection she felt with him.

And then he began to move, and they moved in unison. The intensity of her pleasure climbed and peaked. And she came a second time, and he reached his fulfillment, too, on the heels of her tumultuous climax.

For a time, they held each other close. So close. Senetra was happier that moment than she'd been in years.

"Oh, Senetra." Alex leaned up, taking most of his weight off her. He brushed her hair from her face. "You're absolutely fabulous." He kissed her softly on the lips before he shifted beside her and held her in his arms.

He'd called her Senetra! He knew who she was. She had nothing in her house or on her that referred to that name. Had he known all along?

Senetra tried not to react, but her heart started pounding hard and she hoped he thought it was from their lovemaking, the special moments they'd shared and revealed and not the sound of her name—her real name.

Oh, my God. Did Timothy send him? No. That's impossible. He was Rick's friend. They'd known each other since college.

And he'd said he loved her. And Lord knows she loved him, too.

They always said that a declaration of love in the height of passion was questionable. But she'd spilled her heart and he had seemed real to her.

He couldn't be a private investigator? If he was, then he would have contacted Timothy in March. Senetra was so confused. She needed to get away and think.

Would Timothy meet her at one of their stops? Some of them were so isolated that if he got her, she'd never be seen again. Self-defense classes were all fine and good, but Timothy wouldn't come alone. Not even her attempt at karate could hold out against three or four goons.

"I need to go to my room for a shower and change of clothes. I'm starving. Why don't we meet for dinner in an hour?" she said. "How does that sound?" She tried to sound normal.

"Great." He bent, kissed her deeply before letting her go. Senetra tried to respond normally, but knew she made a weak attempt. He didn't comment on it. Maybe he'd think she was still responding to the aftermath of the orgasm and his declaration of love.

Slipping out of bed, Senetra dressed quickly and at the door she looked back at him. Alex was lying on his back with his hands behind his head, regarding her with a pleased and satisfied look on his face. She smiled at him before opening the door.

For a moment she stood outside his room gathering her breath. She had no time to waste. At least here she could get a plane to Anchorage. She would not go home. But she needed her purse with her ID so she could at least clean out her bank account. She had a contact in

Homer that would get her away quickly if she needed to. But could she go there?

She rushed to her room, not even thinking of taking the time to shower.

Was she doing the right thing? Could Alex have a good explanation for knowing her name and not telling her? He seemed so kind. Someone she thought she could share a future with, the near future at least. Should she just talk to him? But Timothy had seemed nice in the beginning, too. She'd trusted him. People put on fronts all the time. But she'd thought… Could her judgment be that far off—for a second time?

Heck, what did she know? She'd married an abuser. Who said you can't make the same mistake twice? She was looking for all the signs and Alex exhibited none. Maybe… this was her life. She couldn't second-guess it. Timothy had found her before. He would kill her this time. *Damn him.* Senetra stifled frustrated tears. She didn't have time for them. Couldn't she get away from him for a year? One lousy freaking year?

She grabbed her coat and tucked her things in a small bag and left. On her way out the door, she stopped. What if Alex wasn't her enemy? What if he was the man he appeared to be? Then she was doing him an injustice by not trusting him, by running away without talking to him.

She retraced her steps to the bedside table and wrote a short note about having to leave the ferry and left it propped up so that he'd easily see it when he came searching for her. Then she walked out of the room, out the door, looking both ways down the corridor before she closed it after her.

She left the ferry and hoped Alex wouldn't miss her before it pulled from the dock.

Maybe she had enough time to get away. How much, she didn't know. She grabbed a taxi to the local airport.

Home. She couldn't call any place home.

She'd hate to leave the one picture she had of her mother. It was such a tricky set of events that allowed her to teach here. She would not be able to teach again.

She was sick to death of hiding out. If given a chance she'd confront Timothy. But she couldn't reason with a person that mentally unbalanced. She'd have to settle in a new place. Have to find another job—again. Meet new people. Make new friends. How many times would she have to repeat that scene?

Damn it. This was no way to live. No kind of life. She was sick and tired of running. She was sick of just existing. For a little while, she'd been able to glean some pleasure with Alex. Perhaps she could trust him. She just didn't know.

Why should one man have the power to take away her life?

It did no good to ask why, because she had to deal with her reality.

Chapter 12

Dorothelia joined George in the den. They were having a late dinner and George poured a martini and handed it to her. They had a few moments alone before his grandchildren would join them.

"Jasmine and Drake are planning to build a house on the land I pointed out to you yesterday," George said. "They're eager to have their own place." Having them here wasn't a problem. The house was large enough to hold four families without getting in each other's way.

"It's a beautiful piece of property," Dorothelia said. "A wonderful view of the mountains."

"This place will seem empty. I'm used to having the young ones around."

"With the businessmen you're always entertaining here, it'll never be empty."

"Will that bother you? Having people staying, often at the last minute?"

"Not at all."

George sighed and sipped his brandy.

"What's wrong?"

"I was hoping for great-grandchildren before too much longer."

"Both Noelle and Jasmine are newlyweds. They want to spend some time with their husbands before the children begin to come."

"Just wishful thinking."

Dorothelia smiled, reached up and kissed him before patting his jaw. He captured her hand and kissed the back.

"I think it's the perfect time for us to set a wedding date," George murmured.

"But—"

"I know, sweetheart, but the investigator thinks they're getting closer. They've found someone near Seattle who knows of her and he's flying out there in the morning. He thinks it's a good lead."

It was clear Dorothelia wasn't on the same page, but George pressed on. He wasn't a young man and he was eager to begin their life together.

"I think a September wedding will be nice," he said. "It will give him another three months to find her. And it will give us something to look forward to." When Dorothelia remained silent, he said, "Do you have a special preference for the date?" George held his breath, gearing himself up for another argument.

Her chest rose and fell. "September is fine."

George exhaled in relief and kissed Dorothelia's hand again before he tilted her chin and kissed her fully. There was sad acceptance and happiness in her eyes. He wished he could wipe the sadness away, but he didn't want her to go home alone.

"Thank you, darling."

Noelle and Colin came into the room. "None of that," Colin said, and Dorothelia blushed.

"Mind your own business, young man."

George had turned most of the Thoroughbred farm management over to Colin. He was a levelheaded young man and knew the business well. Still, there was a lot of old money involved in it and sometimes a more gentle touch was required. And they had to choose Thunder's mares carefully. You couldn't breed just any filly with a derby-winning Thoroughbred.

Yes, there was plenty of work for both of them.

Of course, with their win at the Churchill Downs, their future appeared to be in terrific shape for the next few years. Fate could intervene, however. No one could forget the tragedy with Barbarossa, which was the reason they weren't taking any chances with their winner.

Stud fees alone would net them many millions.

"Jas and Drake will be down soon," Noelle said.

As they spoke, Jasmine came tearing into the den. "Honest to goodness. That woman. If the meal is two minutes late, she's having a hissy fit."

"Leila is a creature of habit," George said, smiling.

"She should know better by now."

"And you should know better than to talk about me, missy. Or you'll get burned toast for breakfast."

"I take every word back," Jasmine said, kissing Leila on the cheek.

"And don't think I'll melt with a little foolery."

George went to the bar and opened a bottle of champagne.

"What're you doing over there?" Leila asked. "It's time for dinner."

He started filling glasses. "I have an announcement to make," he said, and Leila helped him pass the glasses around. George handed one to Leila. "Have a seat, Leila," he said and joined Dorothelia.

Leila sat on an empty chair with a sigh.

George looked down at Dorothelia. "Dorothelia has agreed to become my bride in September," he said. "You see before you a very happy man. To Dorothelia." He raised his glass.

Everyone shouted congratulations and drank.

"Best wishes," Colin said, coming over to kiss Dorothelia and pat George on the shoulder. "Didn't know you had it in you, old man," he whispered for George's ears alone. And stepped back when George gave him the eye.

"I can still outsmart you, young man, and don't you forget it," George teased with great dignity.

There was a lot of hugging and kissing. Everyone loved Dorothelia. In less than four months, she'd charmed them all.

Leila dug a tissue out of her pocket and blew her nose. "I'm thrilled for you. May you have a lifetime of happiness," she said, before they proceeded to the dining room for dinner.

Leila lagged behind and captured George. "I never thought you'd find someone to love the way you loved Miss Margaret. I meant what I said. I'm very happy for you and she'd be, too. You know she felt life was for the living and she'd want you to move on."

George hugged Leila. She'd been with him more than thirty years and she'd been a godsend. "Thank you, Leila."

"And I'm not retiring. I have many good years left in me."

George laughed. Now in her midfifties, Leila had been a young woman in her early twenties when she began working for him. Her husband had worked on the farm with him, but he'd passed on, too. "You know you have a good retirement settlement from me. I'm not forcing you to leave. I'll leave it to your discretion."

George also knew a romance was blooming with Leila and one of his horse trainers.

"It's time for you to move forward with your romance, too," George said.

Leila sniffed. "You weren't supposed to know about that."

"I know about everything."

She blushed and traipsed to the kitchen.

Alex glanced at his watch and pounded on the door to Senetra's room. She didn't respond. She had to be ready by now, he thought. Even if she wasn't completely dressed, she couldn't be in the shower. He was still puzzled at the way she'd behaved after he revealed his feelings for her. She responded as if she couldn't get out of the room quickly enough.

He knocked again. "Regina, it's me," Alex called out, embarrassed to be yelling in the hallway like some teenager, but when she still didn't respond he got worried.

He searched the lounge area and the restaurant, then toured all the public access areas, but he still couldn't find her.

A half hour later, he discovered that she'd actually left the boat—with a small bag. One of the crew had noticed her leaving in a hurry.

Had she seen someone who frightened her? Why didn't she contact him? She must have known by now he would have protected her.

The ferry was leaving soon. She'd asked him to put both rooms in his name. He got the key to her room. She hadn't taken the time to even pack her luggage. He read the note. She left because of an emergency. What kind of emergency and, again, why hadn't she contacted him?

Quickly, he tossed her things into her suitcase and did the same in his room and left the ship, too. And hoped she'd left a trail he could follow.

He approached the ferry first. He didn't know which direction Senetra was going and she was nowhere around. He had to hope it was home. One ferry had already left. What the heck happened? Had she seen Timothy or someone who could identify her?

He turned it over and over in his mind. Timothy was the only thing that could make her panic that way. Why in heck didn't she tell him if she was in trouble? He just couldn't fathom her leaving under her own steam.

Alex was beginning to panic a little himself. He'd never thought to find a love like Senetra. With the slow pace of the small town, he'd been comfortable and happy with her.

After he checked with the water taxis, he grabbed a cab for the island's small airport.

Senetra missed the plane heading to Anchorage by two minutes. She couldn't believe it as she watched it climb into the air. Two lousy minutes. The next one wouldn't leave until the morning. She could not stay here overnight. No telling what would greet her in the morning.

She'd charter one, then. All of her essential papers were stored in a safe-deposit box in Anchorage. She had to get them before she left. But where would she go from there?

She went into the office. It took her a half hour to find the next plane that was heading to Anchorage. Another couple had chartered it, but they consented to her riding with them. A man and woman back from a fishing trip. Senetra felt safe with them.

The next hour seemed like ten. She tried to sit calmly, but couldn't. She stayed right in the office. She would not leave even to get a sandwich.

Senetra ran over several scenarios, including that Alex could be perfectly innocent. She was taking her flight anyway. When she was out of harm's way in Anchorage, she could sort it all out.

She was walking to the private plane when Alex saw her. Good. He was in time.

"Regina? Wait up. What's going on?"

Fear and anger knotted inside her. He'd found her and he was carrying both their luggage. He dropped the bags on the ground and rushed toward her.

"Stay away from me," she snapped, holding up a staying hand.

He stopped and actually looked confused. Confused? "Tell me what's wrong. What's the emergency?"

"I have to go."

"Let me help you," he said, taking a step forward, close enough for Senetra to see the concern in his face.

"You can't help me."

"Is it something I did?"

"Try this on for size. You lied to me."

He stiffened as though she'd struck him. "I've never—"

"You know my real name," she hissed.

"Your real name?"

She approached him so the others couldn't overhear them. He wasn't going to snatch her right here and run away with her. This wasn't Milwaukee.

"After we made love, you called me by my birth

name. No one knows my real identity, Alex, or is that a fake name, too?"

How could he have done that? Alex thought, at the same time knowing it was easy enough. He always thought of her as Senetra—had always loved that name.

"Can we please talk?" he asked.

"Ma'am, we have to leave now," the pilot said. "I have another pickup."

"I'm asking you to trust me, Senetra. I would never hurt you. I love you. Give me a chance to explain."

"You're asking me to trust you with my life."

"I know." How could he make her believe in him, in what they shared? "Just trust…trust what your heart sees. I'm standing right here before you. You've known me for months. What do you see, Senetra? What have you seen?" he asked. "And what did you see with Timothy?"

Senetra wanted to believe him. She loved him. But if she trusted him and if he was working for Timothy…

She didn't know what to do. She wiped a hand across her face. She gazed at him, studying him.

Then she began to think of the tender ways he'd slowly brought love into her life. The way he'd tried to protect her from Danya, the tender way he touched her, picked clams when all he wanted to do was take her to bed. And this trip, opening her eyes to an Alaska that would have taken her more time to get up the courage to explore. They were on the tail end of their vacation when he'd made the faux pas. And his father. Would a man like that put his own needs aside to save the livelihood of his parent? Was what he told her about that true?

Timothy had been selfish. As much as he'd boasted about what he'd done for her, the things he did weren't for her, but for him.

Senetra rubbed her forehead. Alex went out of his way to open her eyes up to new things. He'd taken the trip. And he didn't have to spend this much time with her to turn her over to Timothy. He could have done that months ago. He wasn't Timothy. They were worlds apart in temperament and actions.

"Ma'am, I have to leave now."

"Tell me your being here has nothing to do with my ex," Senetra said softly, needing to hear the words from him, one last time.

"I don't even know your ex. My presence has nothing to do with him."

She glanced at the pilot. "I've changed my mind," she told him.

Senetra saw the relief on Alex's face and in his stance.

"Let's go to a coffee shop and talk," he said, hailing a cab.

A cab stopped beside them. Ever since the incident, Senetra had been running on adrenaline. As soon as Alex opened the door, her knees buckled and she sank gratefully onto the seat.

They were silent on the short drive. Alex directed the cab to a restaurant they had seen earlier in the day. Although it was after nine, the sun was still bright.

Senetra felt drained. It was all she could do to put one foot in front of the other.

Alex asked for a quiet corner table and the waitress led them across the darkened room. They ordered coffee and just sat peering at the menu with unseeing eyes.

"I've known who you were from the beginning," Alex said without preamble.

"Why didn't you say anything?"

"People don't change their identity for no reason. The obvious reasons are the witness protection program, running from the mob, not that it would work in that case, and spousal abuse. There are many scars on you. I came to the obvious conclusion. Spousal abuse."

"I don't remember meeting you. How do you know me?"

"I saw you at a charity fund-raising function three years ago. I went with my cousin," he said. "The moment I saw you, you took my breath away and I started walking across the room toward you. I wanted to meet you. I was a few yards away, and Timothy approached and escorted you to a couple." Alex shook his head. "I berated myself. You were dripping with diamonds. There was no way I was even in your league."

"Why didn't you tell me all this from the beginning? It would have sav—"

Alex shook his head. "Because you would have bolted, just as you did today. I wanted to give you a chance to know me, to earn your trust. Then I planned to tell you when you were ready to open up to me."

"I wouldn't—"

"You would have left."

Senetra nodded. He was right. She hadn't been ready to date back then, much less trust anyone who knew about her past. Senetra sighed and began to relax enough to read the menu. The waitress arrived with their coffee and they gave her their order.

When the waitress left, Senetra began to tell Alex about her life with Timothy. Halfway through, he moved to her side of the table and put an arm around her shoulder. Taking her hand in his, he rubbed it, giving her comfort.

The more she talked, the more enraged Alex became. He almost wished Timothy was here so he could punch his lights out.

"Did you reveal my name to anyone back home?" Senetra asked when she finished. "My real name?" Obviously, she was still concerned that she might have to move.

"No. They know you by Regina." Alex swallowed hard, warring with his conflicting emotions. He knew she'd had a hard time. But how could she think for a second that he'd turn her over to that piece of scum? Didn't she know him at all?

"How could you ever think I'd harm you? Why didn't you stay and talk to me?"

"Fear of discovery is second nature to me. When you whispered 'Senetra'…there was no way you should have known that name and I just panicked."

"Don't you know I love you? And that I could never hurt you?"

Senetra had to close her eyes briefly against the pain she saw in his eyes.

"I never thought I could feel this way about a man again, but I knew going in that I came with a lot of baggage and that I'd have to live an abnormal life, even though I tried to make it as normal as I could. This thing is not going to leave. Timothy is wealthy and has all kinds of resources," she said.

"A couple of months ago I got a letter from someone back home," she continued. "A private investigator is searching for me. He'll find me eventually. It's impossible to get lost entirely."

"In that case he'll find you any place else you go."

"I know. And I know that I have to stop running at some point. For now I'm safe, but I always have to be aware. An abuser like Timothy isn't going to get 'help.' As far as he's concerned, divorced or not, I belong to him. He won't stop searching until I'm dead. And if you get in the way he could have you killed, too."

"Then we can take care of things once he gets here."

"This isn't the Old West. He won't be open about it."

"Why don't I contact my cousin to find out what's going on? And then we can form a plan from there." Alex squeezed her hand. "You can't run for the rest of your life. At least he can be arrested in Homer. He doesn't have his protection engine in place. His money isn't going to help him there."

Senetra didn't want to be uprooted time and time again. She wanted to settle down. She wanted to be able to call her mother, make sure she was okay. She didn't know how this could end well, but at least she had to try.

She squeezed his hand. "It feels good to be able to share this with someone. I've felt so alone."

"You're not alone, Senetra."

"Don't get me wrong. I'm capable of directing my own life. It's just… Thanks for being here, and I'm sorry I cut your trip short."

"I planned the trip so we could be together. We're near the end anyway."

They checked into a hotel for the evening. It was nine in Homer, six in Milwaukee. While Senetra was in the bathroom, Alex called his cousin, who finally answered on the fifth ring. "This had better be good," he said.

"Hey, stranger," Alex said.

"Alex?"

Alex heard the groan of the mattress as his cousin sat up.

"What're you doing in bed this early?"

"What do you think?" his cousin Pete asked. "Is it really you?"

"It's me," Alex assured him.

"My mom told me you visited your folks for Easter. You should have dropped by here on your way back."

"Didn't have time. But I have a reason for calling you. Do you remember Timothy Blain?"

"Of course I remember him. They gave him a big send-off."

"Send-off? What are you talking about?"

"He's dead."

"Dead?" Alex felt like a parrot. If he was dead, who was searching for Senetra?

"He died in March, man. You need to come home so you can keep up with the news. His girlfriend of the moment killed him while he was dragging her up the stairs to beat the heck out of her," Pete said. "The family is trying to have her prosecuted for his death. She may do some time, but the women's groups are in an uproar. They've gotten her a good lawyer, one that's stressing abuse and that she acted to protect herself. She had a few bruises, but since she never reported any abuse previously, she might have a battle on her hands. You know how popular Timothy was. He knew all the right people."

It sounded like the Timothy Blain Senetra had described, but Alex had to make sure.

"Are you sure Timothy Blain, the one we saw at the benefit, is dead?"

"Of course I'm sure. There have been a million articles in the papers."

"Well, that's news. I'll talk to you later."

Alex shook his head. Could it actually be that simple? His cousin would have no reason to lie to him. He could always look it up on the Internet. Timothy must have died after Alex did the Internet search on him.

When Alex ended the conversation, Senetra was coming out of the bathroom.

"What did you find out?" she asked.

"Timothy's dead."

She stopped in her tracks. "Dead?"

He explained everything in a few quick sentences.

"I can't believe he's been dead since March. But if he's dead, who's searching for me?"

Senetra sat on the bed beside Alex. "Maybe it's my mother searching for me to give me the news."

"More than likely."

"But she wouldn't hire an investigator. I can call her." Senetra took out her cell phone and the room went quiet. She tried her mom's home phone first. Nothing. Then she tried her mother's cell phone and Dorothelia answered on the second ring.

"Mama?" she said, and listened. "It's really me. I just found out Timothy's dead." Tears streamed down her face. She felt horrible for rejoicing in her ex's death, but suddenly a terrible weight lifted from her shoulders as her mother confirmed Timothy's death.

Overjoyed at hearing Senetra's voice, her mother was crying on the other end.

"It's really true. I still can't believe it," Senetra said to Alex, but continued to listen to her mother, who told her she was in Virginia with her donor's father.

After a minute she lifted her mouth from the phone. "She's at my donor father's house and I have two half sisters," Senetra said. "They want me to come to Virginia. My mother's getting married.

"Okay, Mom. I'll catch the morning plane to Anchorage and get a flight from there. I'll call you back with the details." She hung up.

Senetra sat stunned. "I can't believe it."

She knew the constant fear that had become second nature wasn't going to leave immediately.

"We have something to celebrate," Alex said, kissing her.

"It just seems so… All this time he was dead and I was worried that he'd find me."

Chapter 13

Senetra and Alex landed at Dulles and made their way to the luggage carousel. A group of strangers were waiting with her mother. As Senetra ran to Dorothelia with her arms open, she caught a quick glimpse of the distinguished-looking man standing close beside her.

Her mother moved forward. "You're here, really here. You look so good," she said, grabbing her in a tight hug.

"I still can't believe it." Somewhere in the back of Senetra's mind she heard Alex speaking to the people around her, but it all came out in a blur.

She and her mother parted and as they wiped the tears from their eyes they were laughing at the same time. "And no more running. You can come home."

"Oh, my God," Senetra muttered. "I can't believe this. Mom, you look so good." She looked her old self again and there was a different aura around her.

Dorothelia clasped Senetra's face between her hands. "And so do you. You look rested. That weary look is gone. Oh, Senetra." Her mother started to cry again and they were in each other's arms again until they heard a deep chuckle.

"Are you going to share my granddaughter, Dorothelia?" an indulgent voice asked.

Her mother leaned back and wiped her eyes again. "This is your grandfather, Senetra. George Avery."

"Welcome home, granddaughter." George pulled her close to him. He smelled of cherry pipe smoke and warmth.

"Thank you."

"And these are your sisters. Noelle and Jasmine."

Noelle's reddish hair swung around her shoulders, but Jasmine's was cut short. Even though she'd spoken to them the night before, she still couldn't wrap her mind around the fact that she had sisters—that they shared the same paternal genes.

"And their husbands, Colin Mayes and Drake Whitcomb," her mother continued.

There were hugs all around and Senetra was overwhelmed. Coming from such a small family as she did, all these people were unnerving.

Alex had been introduced to everyone except her mother.

"Alex." Senetra beckoned him over. "Mom, this is

my friend Alex Wilson. And this is my Mom, Dorothelia Jackson."

Alex hugged Dorothelia. "It's a pleasure to meet you at last, Mrs. Jackson. Senetra has missed you. She talks about you all the time."

"I've missed her, too."

One moment she was all alone, well, not really alone. The Alaskans had embraced her into the folds of their arms and let her into their families, but now she had real family—sisters and in-laws and a grandfather. She glanced at him again and wondered what to call him. Last night her mother had told her he was marrying her, so he'd be both her stepfather and her grandfather.

Senetra stifled a moan. If she ever told anyone his relationship to her without the history, they'd think she was from one of those mixed-up crazy homes.

Family.

She could live any place she wanted to. She didn't have to hide. There was still shakiness in her limbs. She wondered if she'd ever be able to relax again after her experience with Timothy.

The guys grabbed the luggage and George led the way out of the concourse. The outdoors heat was all encompassing—like being smothered in a damp blanket.

"My God," she said. "Alaska has ruined me. It gets warm in the summer, but I'm not prepared for this. Last night I wore a coat." Senetra was going to scout out a shopping center, and soon. All her clothes were geared to her Alaska trip.

"Quite a difference, isn't it?" her mother said, then whispered, "I like your young man."

Senetra glanced at Alex. He was talking to George. "How can you tell? You just met him."

"He's different. A mother can tell," she said. She'd disliked Timothy from the beginning.

They were hustled into a ten-seat limousine and the driver whisked them toward Middleburg. While acquainting herself with her new family, she gazed at the surroundings. She'd never been to this part of Virginia before, although she'd come to Washington with Timothy for political functions, and she and her mother had vacationed here one summer. But they had stuck mostly to D.C. and the many museums.

"I think this calls for a toast." George pulled out a bottle of champagne. Glasses were filled and passed around.

"My family is together at last."

Alex was given a room next to George's. Senetra's was upstairs.

"I think your grandfather wants to keep me as far from you as possible," he said as they met at the foot of the stairs that evening.

"No doubt," she said, glancing around. "Will you look at this place? My God. What a lovely home." Her bedroom alone was larger than the two bedrooms combined in her apartment. This house was even more elaborate than the one she and Timothy had lived in and he was always taunting her about his upper-crust family and their money. And yet, for all its grandeur, her grandfather's home felt comfortable. *Her grandfather.* She still couldn't fathom it. How eagerly he'd stepped in to find her. Even spent money for an investigator to help a donor child he didn't know existed until a few months ago.

Senetra was saddened that she'd never meet her birth father. If he was anything like his dad, he must have been an amazing man.

"The stables are impressive. He has some prime horses out there," Senetra said.

George beckoned them to a comfortable den. This must be the room he had spent most of his time in. Her mother was already there, and plates of hors d'oeuvres and drinks were already set out on tables.

"I hope you don't mind, dear, but I've taken the liberty of planning a little celebration party this weekend," George said. "Noelle's and Jasmine's families are coming in on Thursday."

A fist clutched in Senetra's stomach. A party? Parties instantly thrust her back to Timothy. Timothy would observe every move she made so that he could complain about them and punish her once they returned home. She still had a ways to go, she realized. Her grandfather was wealthy, but he wasn't like Timothy. She relaxed a fraction. But would he like her?

Senetra sipped on the wine he handed her and smiled her thanks. Before Timothy she never second-guessed herself. She didn't worry about whether the people who should love her would stop if she did the wrong thing or talked to the wrong person or made the wrong comment.

The counselor she saw after she first left Timothy said change and confidence would take a while, but it would come back. Parties in Homer hadn't intimidated her. The people were less formal, everyday people.

"I'm looking forward to it," Senetra said. This was a new day. She was good enough.

"In two days, I'm flying to Milwaukee to see my lawyer. I also asked if he could arrange for me to talk to the lawyer who is representing the woman who killed Timothy," Senetra said.

"Are you sure?" her mother asked.

"If they need me to testify, I will. She must have lived through hell with him."

"I think that's commendable. Dorothelia and I will go with you."

"I appreciate it, but I know you're busy here. I can take care of it."

"But you have to face his family. I don't want you to be alone."

"Alex is going with me," Senetra said. Alex had been a rock. He'd taken another week off to make this trip with her. But she knew she could handle Timothy's family if she needed to.

Senetra spent two days in Milwaukee. Her lawyer informed her that she now owned the house she and Timothy had shared, as well as the rest of his estate. To his family's dismay, he'd refused to change his will.

"Here's the key," her lawyer said.

"I'll go there today," she murmured.

"You don't have to," her attorney informed her. "I can handle everything for you."

She shook her head. "I need to go."

At first she thought she'd never go back to Wisconsin. But she had to know if one of the books her father made for her was still there.

Her hand trembled as she stuck the key in the lock. Alex placed his hand over it. "He can't hurt you anymore."

Senetra nodded and they twisted the lock together. She'd expected things to be different. Different furniture, paintings, antiques. But it was all the same, down to the vase on the foyer table, holding flowers now dried and shedding. The water in the vase had evaporated.

She thought she'd feel—something, but all she wanted was her father's book. It was the only thing she valued in the house.

"My things are still here," she said. Upstairs in the bedroom closet, her lavish designer gowns, suits, shoes, purses and designer luggage still occupied the space as if waiting for her to return.

"My God," Alex said. "Women would kill to have a go at your closet."

"They can knock themselves out," Senetra said, closing the door and going to Timothy's closet where drawers were situated in the center of the room. Their dressing rooms were the size of bedrooms. It was a wonder his family hadn't raided them, but they thought they'd have plenty of time after the reading of the will. Little had they known they wouldn't be allowed in the house again.

"I have to find something. I hope it's here," she said, and began pulling out drawers.

"What are you looking for?" Alex asked.

"My father's book. He made it for me before he died."

Senetra started on one end and Alex on the other. But it wasn't in any of the drawers. In the corner she spotted Timothy's safe. He thought he was so smart in devising a number that no one could determine, but it was their wedding date. She opened it and there was a stack of money and papers, her jewelry—and her father's book.

Senetra glanced through it, page by page, exhaled a long breath and held it against her chest. It was still intact, not one page torn or blemished.

"I have to call his family," Senetra said. "So they can come get some of their son's things if they want them."

"Okay."

Senetra grabbed a breath. Timothy was their proud son. They had thought badly of her when she took out a restraining order and filed for a divorce. They'd probably blame this on her, too, but Senetra knew the truth and so did they, even though they pretended not to. They'd seen her bruises.

But all of this, Timothy and his family, were all in the past now. However, there was one last thing left to do.

Before she left Milwaukee, she would talk with Lidia Smith's lawyer. They wanted to use her as a witness for the defense and she agreed to return for the trial.

She'd have to return, probably more than once, but she could handle it.

Alex and she had made sweet love that night in the hotel, and Senetra was comforted in his arms and by his presence. She glanced at him after he fell asleep, wondering where their relationship would go from here.

And as the plane left for Virginia, Senetra felt freedom she hadn't felt in a long time. Timothy could never hurt her again.

They spent the rest of the week in Virginia and left for Anchorage early Sunday morning.

Alex thought a lot about his relationship with Senetra that week. He'd also thought about the mistakes he'd made with Jessica. Perhaps he should have talked things over with her instead of just ending the relationship. Senetra would spend most of her summer in Virginia. He wouldn't be able to see her as often as he did while she was in Homer.

This time he wanted to do things right. Maybe if he and Senetra discussed their futures together, she'd agree to wait for him, to marry him. He didn't intend to make the same mistake twice.

In Homer they were tucked away in their isolated world. Now the world was hers. She could go anywhere. Would she be satisfied with him? Was their love strong enough?

"Will you spend the day with me in Anchorage and take a later flight out?" Alex asked an hour before their plane landed. They had gotten their seats upgraded to first-class and were enjoying the relative comfort of the larger space. "I've missed you," Alex said.

Senetra smiled, knowingly. "And now you don't have George to intervene."

"It's more than that," he said. "I won't see you for a while. I won't be able to get away next weekend."

"Could I stop here for a few hours on my way to Virginia? Can you get away for a little while?"

He nodded and kissed her hand. At least she planned to continue the relationship—for now.

When they disembarked from the plane, they went to a hotel to store their luggage, and then he took her to one of his favorite restaurants.

"We need to talk about some things," Alex started. So much had happened recently. Maybe now wasn't a good time. But he'd learned to live in the here and now.

The place had a cozy, welcoming atmosphere, and the food was exquisite. They gave their order to the waiter.

"You look serious," Senetra said, placing her napkin on her lap. "I expected you to drag me to bed the second we hit the hotel and not get up for hours."

He didn't respond. Merely took her hand in his.

"I love you, Senetra. Will you marry me?"

"Yes."

Alex blinked. He'd practiced a speech, anticipated her rebuttals and his responses. And she said yes.

"Just like that?" He couldn't believe it.

"I love you. Should I have said no?"

"We have a few things to work out. I don't think we

should announce it until after your mother's wedding."

Senetra nodded. "I agree."

"And I'd still like to work two more years here to fulfill my obligations. After that I should be able to find a job in the D.C. area if you want to live near your family."

"My teaching contract is for two years. I have to be in Homer for that long."

"But I'd don't want to wait two years to marry you," he said. "I'd like to marry next summer."

"Okay."

Alex shook his head. "You're making this too easy for me."

"I know what I want. And I want you. We're living in a time when couples have to deal with long-distance relationships. And that's okay. It's two years out of the rest of our lives."

Epilogue

It was Senetra's wedding day and everyone was running around in a million directions, although it was a very well-organized event. The wedding was being held at River Oaks and it was huge. George had insisted on giving her this day. And it was a grand event from the orchestra to the sit-down dinner that included salmon ordered directly from Alaska and beef directly from Colorado. He'd even brought in a renowned D.C. chef. She chafed at his generosity, but he insisted an Avery wedding had to be done properly.

Although her mother's wedding was perfectly beautiful and grand, George had been more intent on getting married as quickly as possible and didn't have the time to plan anything on this scale. Her mother wouldn't have allowed it anyway.

He and her mother seemed pleased to throw the affair, though. Senetra wasn't as concerned with the pomp and circumstance. Being married to a wonderful man was her main focus. And she had that with Alex. They'd had the year to grow closer and to get to know each other better.

She glanced out the window. The yard was filling up with cars.

"You look beautiful," Jasmine said. "That frilly stuff suits you well." Jasmine preferred plain over ornate.

"I agree," Kathryn said. Kathryn was her maid of honor and her sisters were her bridesmaids.

"Ah, pearls and lace. Just perfect," Noelle said. She was four months pregnant and beginning to show. George was over-the-moon happy about his first great-great-grandchild, not to mention Colin's pleasure. What they didn't know was that Senetra was six weeks pregnant. It wasn't intentional. She'd taken antibiotics after she'd stepped on a nail, and the birth control pill hadn't worked. She'd taken the test a week ago and it was confirmed. Not even Alex knew yet. But he would tonight. She was beginning to feel queasy.

They'd debated buying a house in Homer. But they'd decided it would be easier to live in the apartment until they moved to the D.C. area. She wouldn't have to worry about snow removal or maintenance of a house while he was away. It was a buyer's market and they'd already purchased a house in Virginia and rented it out.

Senetra smiled. Their long-distance marriage would work as well as their long-distance courtship had.

Her mother came into the room looking beautiful after almost a year of marriage. She wore a gorgeous peach gown with an orchid pinned to it.

"It's time, honey. Your grandfather is waiting for you."

Five minutes later she and George stood waiting for the bride's party to proceed up the aisle.

George patted her hand. "You look absolutely stunning," he said.

"You're biased, Granddad."

"Of course. It's still true."

Senetra sighed with nostalgia and pleasure. "This has been quite a year."

"I'll say. I'd like to tell you that I'm very proud of you. And I think you've chosen well in a husband. But also, this is your home. If trouble comes, these doors are always open to you."

She struggled to keep from crying and ruining her makeup. Every time she visited, he spent lots of time with her doing things she'd missed with the absence of a father. He even took her shopping, of all things, when she could afford to buy her own things. She'd balked at that, but taking her shopping gave him pleasure. She remembered that he had no daughters to spoil and Noelle and Jasmine had fathers. So she'd let him buy a few things.

He often took her to lunch, just the two of them. Yesterday, to her mother's annoyance, he'd taken her out of the thick of last-minute wedding preparations and whisked her off to Salamander's with the announcement to her mother that if it wasn't all decided by now, it wasn't going to be.

Senetra smiled. They always went riding together. They'd taken long walks just to talk. And he called at least once a week when she was away.

She kissed his cheek and wiped the lipstick away. "Thank you, Grandpa. For giving me all this. For being there and for making my mother so happy," she said. "And I have a present for you. Alex doesn't know yet. I want to wait until we have a private moment to tell him."

"What is it, dear?"

"I'm pregnant."

George nearly stumbled, but then pulled himself together.

And then the wedding march began. When the door opened George wished he'd had more time to pull himself together. A dignified man couldn't afford to go traipsing down the aisle grinning like a child chewing on a piece of chocolate. Especially with a crowd on both sides of him. The pleasure of escorting his late son's daughter to her new life was reward enough, but now he was going to be a grandfather twice in the space of twelve months.

He contained a sigh of pure joy. Two years ago, he'd been consumed with sorrow. His wife had died; then his son passed, and he knew no greater despair.

He felt like Job, but life had a way of turning. He now had a truly magnificent wife and not one, but three wonderful granddaughters.

The wedding was being held in the garden, and it was bursting with colorful flowers. There were so many guests seated for the wedding that the distance between Senetra and Alex seemed halfway around a racetrack. Alex was standing beside his brother and the groomsmen. He looked fabulous standing beneath the rose arbor in the tux.

The guests stood. Even Iris, Mark and Danya were there. Many of her friends from Homer came. But Senetra's focus was on Alex and the softness in his eyes as he watched her march toward him.

Senetra took his breath away, Alex thought as the noise of the crowd diminished and he could only see her. How had he ended up with a woman so perfect for him? He could not get emotional now. But when her grandfather released her to him, he felt as if he'd been given the greatest gift in the world.

Senetra didn't have to wait very long for Alex's reaction to her pregnancy. They had flown to Paris and were staying in a beautiful and ornate room overlooking the Champs-Elysées and the Eiffel Tower. As he carried her across the threshold, Senetra noticed the balcony and the magnificent view. They walked out there.

It was nighttime and they looked out at the lights.

Later that night, she threw up for the first time.

"Are you sick?" he asked. "Do you think it's something you ate?"

Senetra washed out her mouth. He was standing in the doorway.

"I'm pregnant."

He stood stunned and unable to move. "Pregnant? But you're on the pill."

"Remember when I stepped on the nail and took the antibiotics? It diluted the effectiveness of the pill. Are you disappointed?"

"Disappointed? How can I be? But I'm thinking I need to find a job close to you."

"I'll be fine seeing you on the weekends. We have a plan and we're sticking to it. Besides," she said, rubbing his cheek, "it's just a year."

Alex frowned, clearly uneasy about leaving her alone.

"It'll work out. You'll see."

"We'll discuss that later. I've got other things on my mind right now," he said, rubbing her stomach and gazing at her in awe. He picked her up and carried her back to bed, placing her gently on top.

And there he worked his magic until intense pleasure consumed both of them.

"A wife and a baby," Alex said with great pleasure as he lay back and gathered her into his arms spoon fashion. "All in one day."

REQUEST YOUR FREE BOOKS!

2 FREE NOVELS
PLUS 2 FREE GIFTS!

KIMANI™
ROMANCE

Love's ultimate destination!

KROM10

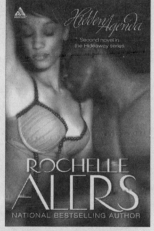

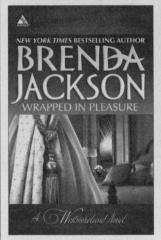